"Do you have a b

Sam barked out a laugh. backup family? No, I'm afraid I don't." What was he going to do now?

"Right. We'll figure something out," Rylee said.

He opened his eyes and lifted his head to stare at this woman. They'd just met and she wanted to help?

Rylee shifted a very content Silas to her other arm. "How would you feel if my family and I helped you out?"

"Are you and your family accustomed to babysitting total strangers?"

One corner of Rylee's mouth lifted in a half smile. "You and I aren't strangers now. Where are you staying?"

"I have a suite at the resort."

"Nice," Rylee said. "Good choice. Most of the out-of-town bridal party is staying there as well. In addition to being your tour guide, would you like me to help you find some reliable childcare?"

What choice did he have other than to accept Rylee's generous offer? "If it's not too much trouble."

But yes. Please help me.

Something indecipherable flashed in Rylee's eyes. "It's no trouble at all."

Heidi McCahan is a Pacific Northwest girl at heart but now resides in North Carolina with her husband and three boys. When she isn't writing inspirational romance novels, Heidi can usually be found reading a book, enjoying a cup of coffee and avoiding the laundry pile. She's also a huge fan of dark chocolate and her adorable goldendoodle, Finn. She enjoys connecting with readers, so please visit her website, heidimccahan.com.

Books by Heidi McCahan

Love Inspired

Home to Hearts Bay

An Alaskan Secret
The Twins' Alaskan Adventure
His Alaskan Redemption
Her Alaskan Companion
A Baby in Alaska

The Firefighter's Twins
Their Baby Blessing
An Unexpected Arrangement
The Bull Rider's Fresh Start

Love Inspired Trade

One Southern Summer

Visit the Author Profile page at LoveInspired.com for more titles.

A Baby in Alaska

Heidi McCahan

LOVE INSPIRED
INSPIRATIONAL ROMANCE

LOVE INSPIRED®
INSPIRATIONAL ROMANCE

ISBN-13: 978-1-335-59862-2

A Baby in Alaska

Copyright © 2024 by Heidi Blankenship

Recycling programs for this product may not exist in your area.

For questions and comments about the quality of this book, please contact us at CustomerService@Harlequin.com.

Love Inspired
22 Adelaide St. West, 41st Floor
Toronto, Ontario M5H 4E3, Canada
www.LoveInspired.com

Printed in U.S.A.

How excellent is thy lovingkindness, O God!
therefore the children of men put their trust
under the shadow of thy wings.
—*Psalm* 36:7

For all those in the aviation industry
who work tirelessly to keep Alaskans safe,
prepared and equipped. Thank you.

Chapter One

Sam Frazier would do just about anything for someone he loved.

But he never imagined that would include becoming the guardian of Silas, his orphaned nephew. He raked his fingers through his hair and paced the floor in his Craftsman-style bungalow on Queen Anne Hill in Seattle. He stopped and stood in a pool of sunlight filtering through the bay windows. Outside, a brilliant blue sky arced over Seattle's iconic skyline, and in the distance, the rugged peaks of the Olympic mountains ringed Puget Sound. Usually the allure of a gorgeous summer Saturday would draw him outdoors. He'd meet up with friends and take the boat out on Lake Washington, or enjoy a long bike ride on the local trails. They'd round out the day lingering over dinner at one of their favorite restaurants overlooking the water.

But he didn't have the luxury of doing whatever he wanted now. Not since his brother and sister-in-law's tragic death in a hiking accident two days ago.

Another peculiar arrow of grief pierced his heart. How could Lucas and Erin be gone? He still couldn't believe it. Sam's breath caught and he battled back the emotion clogging his throat. What was he going to do? He was supposed to travel to Hearts Bay, Alaska, next week. During his three-week stay, he'd serve as best man in a wedding, and he'd agreed to represent his family's interests in the acquisition of a small aviation company on Orca Island. If the deal closed, overseeing the merger was his last commitment with Frazier Aviation, the Seattle-based company his grandfather had started decades ago.

Sam's announcement earlier this year that he planned to leave the family business had created tension. Especially between himself and his father. Dad was not thrilled with Sam's decision. The board of directors respected his dedication to philanthropy, and no one questioned the value of making sure folks in developing nations could access clean water. Sam had tried his best to convey that aviation had never been his thing, and he'd felt called to a new career path that would best use his skills and talents. Advocating for people who couldn't always speak up for themselves was his true passion. But now he'd be pursuing his goals with an infant in tow. He had no clue how he'd juggle it all.

He turned from the window and glanced at the baby boy just six months old, sleeping soundly for now in his vibrating chair contraption on the floor in Sam's den. Poor little fella. Losing his parents at such a tender age. How unfair. Now he had to live with an uncle who was completely inept when it came to babies and parenthood. Their first forty-eight hours together had been rough. Sam had paced the floor with the little guy in his arms, trying everything to console him. Even singing his best off-tune versions of lullabies he barely recalled. Nothing seemed to help. Finally, exhausted and sweaty, Silas had fallen asleep on Sam's shoulder and he'd managed to settle on the corner of his leather couch where they'd clocked a few hours of sleep.

Late last night he'd frantically texted two of his friends who had young children, desperate for advice on how to care for an infant. Sleep when the baby sleeps, you'll find clever ways to get things done, and keep your expectations low had been the main takeaways from his friends' responses. As much as he'd love to take a power nap right now, Silas's peaceful expression propelled Sam into action. He might be a rookie at the guardian thing, but he'd already figured out that his washing machine loads had increased exponentially.

He hurried down the hall to the laundry room and switched the wet clothes from the washer to the dryer. He was supposed to have an emergency conference call this afternoon with Frazier Aviation's board of directors, including his dad, who still functioned as the company's CEO. But Dad had canceled the meeting an hour ago. No explanation was offered. Not that one was needed. Everyone knew it was due to Lucas and Erin's tragic accident. How were they all supposed to carry on with regular operations now? Obviously, they couldn't cancel flights or ground the fleet. Too many commuters and tourists had made reservations and purchased tickets. The company relied on the summer season to generate revenue and turn a profit. Still, it felt surreal to be moving forward with daily operations, not to mention an acquisition in Alaska, knowing Lucas and his wife were never coming back.

Sam closed the dryer door, hit the proper buttons, then returned to the kitchen and sank into a wooden chair at his small round table. This time tears stung his eyes and he didn't bother to resist. He rested his elbows on the walnut surface and buried his face in his hands. He'd never play another game of disc golf with his big brother, Lucas. Or tease him about his life-long obsession with baseball cards. Lucas and Erin had been a fantastic couple. She'd been a pediatric heart surgeon and Lucas had been the CFO of Frazier Aviation. Sam was certain their father had expected Lucas to take over the company in the near future.

His body trembled and sorrow washed through him as he grieved for all their family had lost. All that sweet Silas had lost. Sam still couldn't wrap his mind around how Lucas and Erin hadn't returned home from their weekend adventures in the North Cascades. Lucas had been hiking in those mountains for most of his life. He and Sam had camped at a state park there late last summer. It seemed nearly impossible that Lucas and Erin had both slipped and fallen to their deaths.

But questioning his family's heartbreaking reality wouldn't change anything. Somehow, they'd have to muster the strength to move on. Sam swiped at the tears on his cheeks with the back of his hand, then silently whispered a prayer.

Lord, why did they choose me? I don't have

any experience with children. I've never even dated a woman who had a kid. There has to be someone who'd be better for Silas. I'm lost. Please. Help me.

The room remained quiet other than the steady hum of the dryer. He would figure this out. One step at a time. Pushing to his feet, he went into his office at the end of the hall, pulled out a pad of paper and scrawled out a to-do list. The first action item? Find a nanny in Alaska for the wedding. He'd considered backing out on being the best man. Given the sudden death of his brother and sister-in-law, and his new responsibility for Silas, telling his buddy Josh that he couldn't make it wasn't unreasonable. But they'd been close friends since college, and Josh wanted very much to marry his beautiful bride-to-be Crystal in her hometown of Hearts Bay. It seemed serendipitous that Sam had planned to head that way for the acquisition. But now, with Lucas and Erin gone, maybe he shouldn't be traveling. Maybe what Silas needed was the solid, routine comfort of home.

His phone hummed on the desk. A text from Josh filled the screen.

Hey, man. I'm just checking on you. So sorry to hear about your brother and Erin. That's horrible. Is there anything I can do? Please let me know.

Sam's fingers hovered over the keyboard. He typed, then deleted, typed, then deleted his text again. If he was going to back out on being the best man in Josh and Crystal's wedding, he couldn't share that news in a text message. Besides, he didn't feel a sense of peace about bailing on his friends. He'd done a lot of extraordinary things in his life. Skydived, and summited a handful of mountain peaks in North America, and helped people dig wells in remote locations globally. Surely he could figure out how to travel to an island in Alaska with an infant. Right?

Maid of honor. Seriously? There had to be somebody else. *Anybody* besides her.

"I don't know, Crystal. Are you sure you don't want to ask Chelsea instead? She loves planning showers and all that girlie stuff." Rylee Madden tried not to let her facial expression reveal her panic.

Crystal Gatlin's flawless brow crimped with disappointment. "Come on, Rylee. Please say yes. I know it's short notice, but you were my bestie when we were young. Why wouldn't I ask you?"

Rylee hesitated, propping her phone against the can of diet soda on her desk. The can she'd been about to open and enjoy before Crystal called on FaceTime and made her surprise request. It was sad that Crystal's sister had been put on bed rest, but she still didn't understand why Crystal wanted Rylee to take her place. "I… I've just never been a maid of honor before, that's all."

Okay, so that was a lame response. Crystal's eye roll indicated she'd felt the same way.

"It's not that hard. You're already a bridesmaid. Now you'll just have a couple of additional responsibilities. Since my sister won't be able to come to the wedding, I need you to step up. Chelsea's sweet and all, and I'm glad she's a bridesmaid, but you and I have always been closer."

"Does Josh have a sister?"

Crystal frowned. "He does, but she's not going to be my maid of honor. We're not close. What's wrong? You love parties and having a great time. Why are you being so weird about this?"

"I do love parties." Rylee sighed. "It's just that—"

"Wait. Is this about Tucker?"

"No, of course not." Rylee forced a laugh. "That was over ages ago."

She had thought Tucker had been the one. He'd come to Hearts Bay with friends to go fishing at one of Orca Island's remote locations.

They'd started talking when she'd flown him and his buddies out to the lodge. The following week, they'd run into each other at Maverick's. A conversation turned into dinner and all of a sudden he'd decided he could work remotely from Hearts Bay. Her family had cautioned her to take things slow.

Except, she'd never been the cautious type. And like a fool, she'd introduced him to her beautiful cousin who'd been visiting from out of town. A few weeks later, Tucker and her cousin had up and moved to Texas. They'd left her behind to piece the jagged fragments of her wounded heart back together.

"Rylee? Hello?"

Yep, she'd zoned out. "I'm still here."

"The good news is, there are single eligible men in the wedding party." Crystal smiled. "In fact, I think you and the best man would totally hit it off."

"Hold on." Rylee lifted her palm toward the phone. "Please do not try to set me up. I'm not interested."

"You're not interested in meeting someone new?"

"I didn't say I wasn't interested in meeting someone new. I don't want to be set up with someone who will be leaving town after the wedding. Long-distance relationships don't end well. Besides, I'm super busy at work. I don't have time to start a new relationship right now."

"Do you still have time to be in my wedding?" Crystal pooched out her lip in a pouty expression.

Rylee stifled a groan. When did Crystal become so melodramatic? "I will absolutely be in your wedding. I'm not sure I'm the best fit for maid of honor, but I am very flattered that you asked. And if that's what you need, I can do my part to make your day feel extra special."

Oh, boy. That was a significant promise. Could she afford to keep it? "Is July fourteenth still the big day?"

"You know it." Crystal's pout instantly transformed into a dazzling smile.

"Wow. Time is flying. That's less than three weeks away."

"I know, right? And there's still so much to do. Especially now that my sister can't be there."

"She needs to take care of herself and those sweet babies." Rylee grabbed a pen and a receipt from her last trip to The Trading Post. "So when will you be back in town?"

Crystal gave Rylee the date for her arrival from Anchorage, details about what Rylee needed to know regarding the rehearsal dinner, and the venue for the bridal shower. They said goodbye and Rylee ended the call.

She set her phone facedown on the desk and blew out a long breath. "Oh, my."

Carson, her coworker at Hearts Bay Aviation, shot her a curious glance from behind the front counter. "Everything okay?"

"I was just coerced into being maid of honor in my best friend's wedding."

His brows sailed upward. "Isn't that something you normally would get some advance notice about?"

"Usually. But the bride's sister is pregnant with twins and can't be in the wedding party. So the responsibility is now mine."

Carson looked at the clock. "I don't mean to be insensitive, because I know you have a lot on your mind, but are you still up for that mail run?"

"Oh, right." Rylee stood then pushed back her chair and grabbed her phone and her backpack. "I'm on it."

"Good," Carson said. "The mailbags are loaded and you're all set."

"Thanks for the reminder." She high-fived him on her way out the back door.

Outside, mottled clouds dotted the June sky. Perfect flying weather. She strode across the asphalt to the hangar. Ever since their boss,

Paul Sutton, had announced he was retiring and moving to Nevada, life had been stressful for the small staff of pilots working at Hearts Bay Aviation. The news that Paul intended to sell the business and they'd most likely be acquired by a larger family-owned operation out of Seattle had left her and Carson and their colleagues on edge.

She loved her work. Flying to villages that didn't have roads. Battling the elements. She'd moved freight, people, mail, animals, whatever needed to be handled. She and her trusty Cessna got the work done. She enjoyed the freedom of soaring over the rugged mountains and intricate coastline of Alaska. Every single flight gave her another opportunity to appreciate her home state's breathtaking beauty. Since she'd learned to fly as a teenager, she'd relished the challenge of being the only female pilot working for a small business. Other than Paul's wife, Libby, who ran the front office, the rest of Paul's employees were men.

Uncertainty slid its icy fingers around her insides and gave an unwelcome squeeze. Would her job change after they were acquired? If Frazier Aviation made an offer and Paul accepted, would they bring in a whole new staff of their own pilots from out of state? Her boss had tried to reassure them that they had no reason to worry about job security. But he wasn't going to be the one flying for these people. What if they terminated her position? What if she had to move to Anchorage and find a new job with one of the regional airlines?

Rylee pushed those unsettling questions aside and began her preflight safety check.

A trip out to this particular remote village was one of her favorite routes. Especially since, if the weather permitted, she could catch a ride up the hill to visit her grandmother, who still lived independently at the age of eighty-seven. Rylee and her family had tried numerous times to bring her into town. They'd even built a house for her on her parents' property, but Grandmother wouldn't hear of moving.

Rylee opened the door to the plane's cockpit and climbed inside. Her thoughts turned to her conversation with Crystal. The request to step in as maid of honor had thrown her for a loop. She wasn't proud of the way she'd reacted, either. It had been almost a year since Tucker had shredded her heart and run off with her cousin.

Shouldn't she be over it by now? Being an adult meant putting her own issues aside and celebrating Crystal and Josh's big day.

She could do this. She'd find a way to be happy for one of her dearest friends. She'd find a way to care about all the stuff she was supposed to care about. What was a maid of honor supposed to do again? All that came to mind was fluffing the veil and adjusting Crystal's train. There had to be more than that. She'd ask her sisters. They'd all been in plenty of weddings. Her sister Lexi had worked weddings as a photographer. Hopefully she'd have some key tips to share.

She'd fulfill her duties as the maid of honor but she was not falling for that best man. Even if he was the smartest, most clever, charming guy to venture onto the island. Crystal would have to let go of her matchmaking plans. Because Tucker had taught her a painful lesson—she'd rather stay single than hurt like that ever again.

Oh, this was not going well at all. Silas released another angry wail. Would he ever stop crying? How did a small human make such a heartbreaking sound?

Sam adjusted the canvas cover on Silas's car seat and exited the plane. Rain pelted Sam's face as he made his way down the steep wet stairs and onto the tarmac outside Hearts Bay's tiny airport. At least they'd flown on a twin-engine jet from Anchorage. When they'd left Seattle before dawn this morning, he'd envisioned making the last leg of their all-day journey on a prop plane. Thankfully, that hadn't been the case.

Not that it made any difference to a baby. The little fella's mournful cries drew a curious glance from the young man who'd marshaled the aircraft to a standstill. Sam let his gaze slide away. It had been eight days since his brother and sister-in-law had passed. Sam had hoped that his nephew's almost constant crying would lessen by now. Maybe that was selfish, though. Sam's heart squeezed. He was still in the throes of grief himself. How could he expect a baby to not miss the two people who had met all his needs? Sam vowed for at least the fifth time today to lower his expectations. Surely this stage would pass. But what then?

He gripped the spongy foam handle on the car seat as it bumped against his leg. With his other hand, he awkwardly shifted the weight of his heavy bag, struggling to keep it draped over his shoulder. Ribbons of fog wound around the island's lush green mountainside. The red lights of a plane taxiing by blinked in the gray afternoon. He couldn't remember the last time he had exited a plane from a set of airstairs. This airport was much smaller than he'd anticipated. Maybe there was more than one airport on Orca Island. Even though numbers and data were his thing and he'd spent hours poring over the documents, the minute details of this acquisition escaped him now. Too many nights in a row without sleep did that to a person. Oh, well. There would be plenty of time to revisit all of that later.

He had to collect their luggage, load the rental car and get to the resort. Then he'd track down the nanny he'd hired over social media, and maybe together they could get Silas on a reasonable routine for the next three weeks.

Pungent fumes from the aircraft's engines wafted toward him. The luggage carrier rattled by. Sam sidestepped a puddle of water on the asphalt. The man in rain gear and a bright orange safety vest driving the cart offered a smile and a friendly wave. Sam grimaced. He appreciated the kind gesture, but, man, he was in a mood. The loss of Lucas and Erin, lack of sleep, and the intense stress of taking care of an infant when he had exactly zero experience with babies was taking a toll.

Trying to hire a nanny and pack for himself and a baby to attend a wedding and business meetings had been too much. Not to mention this kid just did not sleep. Sam's nerves were frazzled. Squinting against the rain and the wind blowing at him, he managed to get to the entrance leading into the airport. The automatic doors parted and he stepped inside.

Oh, wow. He'd been in lakefront homes bigger than this. He surveyed the ticket counter, a few offices tucked in the opposite corner, and a minuscule baggage claim area with two conveyor belts. A basic security checkpoint separated the gates from the airport's front doors.

Sam followed the other passengers from his flight past the stanchions and canvas ropes marking off the arrival zone. He stopped beside a beautiful mural painted on the wall featuring a brown bear, a deer and a bald eagle and pushed back his hood on his anorak. Silas finally stopped crying. Sam was afraid to move for fear he'd provoke more tears. He gently lowered his bag to the floor, then set Silas's car seat down beside it.

A woman with long sleek brown hair and the most beautiful golden-brown eyes he'd ever seen approached. She wore a bright blue jacket with a vaguely familiar logo emblazoned on the front panel, jeans and work boots. His eyes traveled to the piece of paper she held with his name printed in black marker.

"Sam Frazier?"

He offered a polite nod. "Yes."

She lowered the piece of paper. "I'm Rylee Madden. I work for Hearts Bay Aviation. My boss sent me over to meet you. Welcome to Orca Island."

"You're Rylee Madden?"

Her smile faltered. "Let me guess. You were expecting a man?"

Warmth heated his skin. "No. I mean I just thought—"

"Relax." Her tight expression conveyed her annoyance. "Happens all the time. Unfortunately, my boss is out of town helping his daughter and grandkids move. He asked me and my coworker Carson to show you around."

"Yeah, about that. There's been a slight change of plans. I have a baby with me."

Her gaze slid to Silas in his car seat. "So I noticed."

"I'm also in town for a wedding, so I've kind of got a lot going on."

"We'd better hustle then. Baggage claim is right this way." She turned on her heel and strode to the opposite end of the room.

Sam squeezed his eyes shut. *Way to go, Frazier. It took you all of three minutes to behave like a pushy, entitled jerk. Super.*

He opened his eyes and leaned down to grab the car seat. Silas stared up at him, one finger jammed in the side of his mouth. Tears clung to his long dark eyelashes. The kid was probably appalled by Sam's behavior.

Sam blew out a breath, then spoke softly to the boy. "I know. That wasn't my best moment, was it? I'll have to try to do better. Come on, let's go find the sixteen pieces of luggage I had to bring to keep you happy."

He shouldered his bag and slogged toward the conveyor belts, his muscles aching from the awkward job of toting an infant car seat and an overstuffed carry-on.

He stopped near Rylee and scanned the suitcases and duffel bags gliding by. None of them looked like anything that belonged to him. Hopefully, everything had made the connection in Anchorage.

Rylee glanced up from her phone. He couldn't help but notice the appealing pink clinging to her cheekbones. Or the cross-shaped pendant on her necklace that nestled in the hollow at the base of her throat.

"Are you here for Josh and Crystal's wedding?"

He forced himself to meet her gaze. "I am."

"Small world. Crystal just asked me to be the maid of honor."

A pleasant pang of surprise tapped at his insides.

"But you're also here representing Frazier Aviation, right? For the acquisition?"

Sam lowered the car seat to the floor once again and palmed the back of his neck. "Yes. We've had a tragedy in the family, so I agreed to follow through on the acquisition since I was already here for the wedding. There's—"

Silas released the most heartrending screech, interrupting his explanation and drawing Rylee and Sam's attention immediately. Silas arched his back and strained against the car seat buckles. His face turned red and crumpled with despair.

Sam cast a nervous glance toward the baggage claim, where his first suitcase had just slid down the shoot and onto the belt. How was he supposed to collect all of his stuff when Silas was screaming? He couldn't just leave him there in his car seat. Besides, he hadn't even taken the time to rent a luggage cart yet. Did they have those here? He turned in a circle, looking around for a solution. Panic welled inside, making his heart race.

"Would you like me to hold him?" Rylee tucked her phone in the back pocket of her jeans, then sank to her knees on the tile floor. "What's his name?"

"Silas."

"Hi, Silas," she cooed. "Is it all right with you if I unbuckle him?"

"Absolutely." Sam managed to push the word past his dry throat.

"Come here, sweet boy." She released the clips and scooped Silas out of the car seat. After nestling him against her shoulder, Rylee stood slowly. "He's very cute."

"Uh, thanks, but he's not actually mine."

Rylee shot him an alarmed look. "What?"

Oops. That didn't come out quite right. "It's not what you think. I'm his new guardian. Silas is my nephew. His parents passed away recently."

Rylee's face fell. "Oh, I'm so sorry."

She patted Silas gently on his backside with her palm and swayed gently. Back and forth in a way that some people just naturally seemed to know how to do. Sam couldn't avert his eyes. He felt ridiculous whenever he tried to sway while attempting to comfort Silas. Maybe he just needed more practice.

"You do have a lot going on."

Sam reached for his own phone. "That's why I hired a nanny to help out while I'm here."

Rylee stopped swaying. "You hired a nanny? In Hearts Bay?"

Her tone gave him pause. He glanced up from his phone. "Is there something wrong?"

"If you don't mind me asking, who did you hire?"

Sam opened his email, scrolled and then shared the name with her.

"Oh, dear." Rylee's nose wrinkled.

Sam's stomach plummeted to the tips of his

expensive hiking boots. "Don't tell me I made a poor decision."

"Well she left on the morning flight. I watched her check in." Rylee chewed her lip and shrugged her slender shoulders. "Maybe she had an emergency."

"That's ridiculous." Sam scrolled quickly through his recent emails, then his texts. "She didn't tell me."

"Do you have a backup plan?"

Sam barked out a laugh. "A backup nanny? No, I'm afraid I don't." He let his eyes close and dropped his chin to his chest. What was he going to do now?

"Right. Okay then. We'll figure something out."

He opened his eyes and lifted his head to stare at this woman. They'd just met and she wanted to help?

Rylee shifted a very contented Silas to her other arm. "I know this is a bit outside the box, but how would you feel if my family and I helped you out?"

"Are you and your family accustomed to babysitting total strangers?"

One corner of Rylee's mouth lifted in a half smile. "You and I aren't strangers now. My family does have a history of welcoming people into their home. It's a long story. Where are you staying?"

"I have a suite at the resort."

"Nice," Rylee said. "Good choice. Most of the out-of-town bridal party is staying there, as well, and I have siblings on the island with lots of connections. In addition to being your tour guide, would you like me to help you find some reliable childcare?"

Sam hesitated. He glanced down at his phone and scrolled through the email and texts one more time. There was nothing from the young woman who'd promised she'd start watching Silas tomorrow. What choice did he have other than to accept Rylee's generous offer? "If it's not too much trouble."

But, yes. Please help me.

Something undecipherable flashed in Rylee's eyes. "It's no trouble at all."

Chapter Two

What was she *doing*?

Rylee wedged the portable crib between a duffel bag and a suitcase in the back of the SUV Sam had rented.

She'd never been a baby person. Unofficially designated the fun aunt in the Madden family, she was always quick to play a game of tag or jump on the trampoline in her parents' yard. If her nephew Cameron did well on a test or school project, she'd take him out for dough-nuts or a smoothie at The Trading Post. And if there was a special occasion to celebrate, she'd be the first to plan the party or make the res-taurant reservation. But she was definitely not the girl who soothed a cranky infant or showed up with crackers and lemon-lime soda when a virus circulated around Hearts Bay.

But she'd taken one look at Sam Frazier

with his raven-black hair and clear blue eyes and made up her mind right then to help him. The grief clinging to the lines around his eyes and mouth, not to mention that heart-wrenching story he'd shared about losing his brother and sister-in-law had blasted through her previous misconceptions. Sam was the opposite of a high-powered aviation executive and not at all whom she'd anticipated meeting today. All of her intentions to remain stoic and detached had melted like a snowbank in the spring sunshine once she'd realized how much he struggled with comforting Silas.

"Here you go. This is the last of it." She handed him yet another piece of baby equipment from the luggage cart they'd loaded down and pushed out into the parking lot. She held on to the edge of her hood, hunching her shoulders against the cold drizzle.

"Thank you." Sam closed the passenger door and met her near the vehicle's open hatch.

He'd just finished securing baby Silas in his car seat in the middle row of the SUV. Evidently, Sam had given up on wearing his hood because his dark hair was soaked and clinging to his head. Poor guy. He'd had a long day already.

"My invitation still stands. Would you like to join our family for dinner?" Rylee clutched the handle on the luggage cart to keep it from rolling away.

Sam's handsome features crimped. "I don't know. We're worn out. I think we should just get to the resort and settle in for the night."

"Are you sure? We'll feed you a hot meal and I promise there will be at least one extra set of experienced hands to help with the baby."

Oh, boy. She pinched her lips tight. He probably wouldn't appreciate her implying that he couldn't handle a meal and caring for his nephew, something he'd likely been attempting for at least a few days now. Except he didn't appear confident. And he and Silas were both exhausted.

Sam plucked his phone from the inside pocket of his jacket. "It's not even six o'clock yet. Silas will likely be grouchy for the next couple of hours. This is usually a tough time of day."

"The resort has decent room service, but if you don't want to eat alone with a grouchy baby, I'm more than happy to let you follow me to my parents' place."

"Since you put it that way, I'm almost afraid to say no." Sam's tired smile provoked a surprising flutter in her chest. What was going on? A charming smile was all it took to make her heart take notice? That seemed like a recipe for disaster. She'd have to work on that.

"If you give me your phone, I'll put my name and number in, then text you the directions. It's not far."

Thankfully, the rain tapered off and Sam handed her the phone. She quickly input her contact information and gestured toward her vehicle parked a few spaces away. "I'm driving that silver pickup truck."

He took his phone back and glanced over his shoulder. "Great. I'll be sure to follow you."

"See you there." Rylee jogged across the parking lot to her vehicle. After she settled inside, turned on the engine and the windshield wipers, she fished out her phone and texted Sam the address and specific directions to her parents' house on the island. He acknowledged the text with a quick thank-you. The next message she sent was to the family group text chain. She had to let them know that tonight's gathering included guests. Her sisters would probably ask for more details. Not that she'd respond. No reason to keep Sam and Silas waiting. Her family would have their curiosity satisfied in less than fifteen minutes.

She still couldn't believe Sam was the best man in Crystal and Josh's wedding. What an interesting turn of events. Not that she was changing her mind about a new romantic relationship. Crystal's pie-in-the-sky idea that she could play matchmaker with members of her own bridal party didn't sit well. Sure, Crystal and Josh had found one another, but that didn't mean everyone else they knew had to pair off. Happily-ever-after wasn't for everyone.

Rylee slowly drove out of the airport parking lot, checking in her rearview mirror to make sure Sam was following. Poor Silas. Dragged to Alaska and mourning the loss of his parents and everything that was familiar. Those tears clinging to his eyelashes and his pathetic cries had tugged on her heartstrings. Then he'd snuggled on her shoulder and she'd breathed in his sweet scent and before she could even think twice, she'd offered up her family's babysitting services.

They didn't know that yet. She'd have to corral Mom in the kitchen and share the update. Because between her commitments to Crystal, showing Sam around Hearts Bay, and managing her usual workload, there wasn't much wiggle room in her schedule to be a nanny.

As she tapped the accelerator and picked up speed, cruising down the road toward her family's place, the rain tapered off and the gray clouds parted. Beams of sunshine broke through and bounced off the blue-green water lapping at the island's rugged coastline. If Sam had lived in Seattle for any length of time, he'd probably grown accustomed to damp weather. A little sunshine would be nice, though, especially if her family went outside after dinner.

Rylee had always been so passionate about flying and creating a life that she loved for herself in Alaska that she'd never felt the need to marry, settle down and start a family. Some of her high school classmates had been married for several years already and had children. She was almost thirty years old. Plenty of time yet. But she'd fallen so hard and so fast for Tucker, and he'd given her a glimpse of what a future together might look like.

Then yanked it all out from under her like a cruel prank.

She'd spent months since he'd left town with her cousin fortifying the walls around her heart. Determined not to foolishly allow anybody to woo her like that again.

But meeting Sam had been nothing like meeting Tucker. When she'd held little Silas for the first time and heard Sam's family's tragedy, suddenly he wasn't the face of the company responsible for acquiring her boss's business. Instead he was a grieving human trying to provide for his nephew. And she knew a thing or two about grief. The loss of her brother, Charlie, and his best friend Abner in a fishing accident eight years ago had changed her life forever.

Slowing down to make the turn onto the road leading to her parents' place, she glanced in the mirror again to make sure Sam was still there. His white SUV trailed her truck at a respectful distance. Through the trees, she glimpsed the roof of her childhood home. A refuge on the edge of the island overlooking the same ocean that had claimed Charlie's and Abner's lives. It was a strange thing, loving a body of water that had taken so much.

Charlie had taught her everything she knew about fishing, berry picking and hiking. They'd often joked about buying a lodge in one of the most remote parts of the island. She'd fly in their guests and Charlie would take them for epic fishing adventures. Even though that dream had evaporated when Charlie had passed, Rylee's love for Orca Island had grown exponentially through the years.

It wasn't easy being a female aviator in a profession dominated by men. Layer in the additional challenges of flying on and off an island in the middle of the ocean, and she'd be the first to admit there had been some white-knuckle landings. But she'd learned to hold her own. She couldn't imagine living anywhere else.

So, yeah, Sam Frazier might be handsome

and his family owned a reputable aviation business, but she was only offering a helping hand because Silas needed her. She didn't have a heart of stone, despite Tucker's treatment causing her to fortify her defenses.

Or maybe it was Sam who needed the help. He'd behaved like a fish out of water since the moment she'd spotted him at the airport. Either way, she'd step up and do her part. After she showed him around the island, introduced him to the business manager at work, and they celebrated Crystal and Josh's wedding, then Sam and Silas would go back to their lives in Seattle. Because that's just how it was with handsome men who made summer stops in Hearts Bay. They loved to visit but never as much as they loved to leave.

"So is your family serious about this acquisition?" Gus tossed another log on the fire and then pinned Sam with a long look.

Sam shifted in his canvas chair. Gus's piercing gaze unnerved him. They'd only met a couple of hours ago. Now they sat beside each other in the Maddens' backyard. Sam wasn't prepared to talk shop. Gus hadn't said much during dinner. Was he a pilot? Did he work for a competing airline? Or maybe just a good guy looking out for Rylee's best interests.

Stalling, Sam looked around. The storm that had greeted him when he'd arrived in Hearts Bay earlier today had dissipated, making way for a pleasant evening. Flames snapped and crackled from the fire pit, sending a tendril of smoke into the cool air. The mountains across the water were silhouetted against a pale blue sky dotted with wispy pink clouds.

Gus kept staring. Patiently waiting for a response. Sam wasn't sure if it was Gus's imposing presence, fatigue, or the fog of grief that he was still swimming through that made him spill the truth, but he decided to be completely honest. "My father expects me to close the deal while I'm here. Personally, I'm more interested in clean water."

"Sorry?" Gus's chair creaked as he leaned forward and prodded the smoldering log in the fire with a long stick.

"I'm a financial analyst for my family's company. They've been in the aviation industry for years in the Seattle area. Earlier this year, I announced I was stepping away to pursue my passion, which is making sure people in other parts of the world can access clean water." Sam forced his mouth into a weary smile. "That news didn't go over well, so I agreed to oversee this acquisition. Sort of my last hurrah, if you will."

"How's that working out for you so far?"

"It's complicated." Sam reached for the bottle of water he'd set in the chair's cup holder. He'd already explained over dinner how he'd come to be Silas's guardian. It wasn't a story he cared to rehash again.

Sam took a sip of water and soaked in his surroundings. He had anchored on luxury vessels in the middle of Lake Washington, sat on Caribbean beaches and watched gorgeous sunsets, and hiked to the summit of some of the most breathtaking mountains on the continent. But this island community rivaled anything he'd ever seen.

"So when you say clean water, you don't mean municipal water supply? You aren't transitioning into urban planning, right?" Gus asked.

Sam twisted the cap back on the water, sat up straighter, and met Gus's gaze. "Listen. I'm exhausted and probably starting to babble. I don't blame folks for being curious about why I'm here. There are no secrets."

Gus's brows knitted together, but he allowed Sam to keep speaking without interrupting.

"To answer your original question, Frazier Aviation is quite serious about this acquisition. But it was my brother, Lucas, who had a passion for flying. He followed in Dad's footsteps in the company. For a few years, I was happy to be involved in the financial aspect of things. But I've realized I'm much more interested in raising money and giving it away so that people in developing nations can have access to functioning wells and clean water. Women and children can spend time learning to read and communicate effectively rather than spend hours hauling dirty water that just makes them sick."

"Right on." Gus nodded. "That's fascinating. So you're here to manage this acquisition and be the best man in the wedding?"

Before Sam answered, the back door opened and closed. Rylee strode across the yard, carrying Silas in her arms. "Okay, little mister is fed and wearing clean clothes and a new diaper. Hope you don't mind that we put him in some pajamas that we found in his bag."

"Thank you very much." Sam rose to his feet. "You didn't have to do all that."

"As I said earlier, there are lots of extra hands here. People want to be helpful. Besides, we know you're probably worn out." She passed Silas to him. The baby's eyelids were heavy and he yawned as Sam awkwardly settled him in the crook of his elbow. Rylee's fingers brushed against his as she pulled away. A pleasant sensation zipped up his arm and across his shoulders. Boy, he must've gone too long without dating anyone if touching an attractive woman's hand distracted him like that.

"Thanks again for everything," Sam said. "You all have been real lifesavers tonight."

Gus smiled for the first time since they'd met. "You'll find that the Madden family is quite good at coming to the rescue."

Sam leaned over and extended his hand. "It's great meeting you, Gus. Hope to see you around."

Gus gave Sam's hand a bone-crushing squeeze. "Same."

Sam turned away so Gus didn't see him grimace.

Rylee met his gaze. Her eyes sparkled with amusement. Did she notice that Gus had almost hurt him? How embarrassing.

"I'll walk you out to your car," Rylee said. "Do you need help grabbing anything from inside?"

Gone were the days of leaving the house quickly with keys, a phone and his wallet. Would he ever get used to how much equipment one baby required? Their visit to Orca Island made him feel even more out of sorts.

"You've done so much already," Sam said, carefully shifting Silas to his other shoulder. "I can swing by and grab our stuff. I'd like to thank your parents for hosting us tonight anyway."

Silas cooed softly. Sam glanced down at him and smiled. Silas hadn't cried since Rylee had carried him outside. As they walked across the Maddens' lush green lawn, the shouts of the kids bouncing on the trampoline filtered through the air.

"My parents left on a walk together. It's a new routine they started recently. You'll probably pass them on the road."

"Perfect," Sam said. "I'll be sure to stop and thank them."

A few minutes later, after Sam had passed through the house and grabbed the bag he'd used to carry Silas's stuff, he met Rylee beside his SUV in the Maddens' driveway.

He opened the back door, set the bag on the floor, and carefully maneuvered Silas into his car seat. The little fella was probably beyond exhausted. He fussed as Sam carefully latched the buckles on the five-point harness then tucked a small blanket with ribbon loops stitched on the edge over Silas's legs. It was one of the few items that seemed to bring the baby comfort.

"We gave him a pacifier when he was inside with us," Rylee said. "It's in the outside pocket on your bag. Do you want to try and see if he'll take it?"

"Absolutely." He'd try anything to keep Silas content. Sam reached inside the pocket, found the pacifier and offered it to Silas. He started sucking immediately and his eyelids fluttered closed.

"Wow." Sam stared at him. "Is it really going to be that easy?"

Rylee chuckled. "I hope so. You deserve a peaceful ride to the resort. Do you need directions?"

"No, I have them in my email confirmation." Sam gently closed the door and turned to face her. "Thank you. I know I keep saying this, but you and your family have been extremely generous. You've made a difficult situation so much more bearable."

She dropped her gaze and dragged the toe of her boot across the pebbles in the driveway. "We like to be helpful around here. I hope we haven't been too overbearing."

"Are you kidding? I obviously need a lot of guidance."

Rylee tipped her chin up. A smile tugged at the corners of her lips. "That's good to hear because I've already texted you tomorrow's itinerary. I have a fitting for my bridesmaid dress in the morning, but I could meet you after that and give you a tour of the island."

"Right. The tour." Sam massaged his forehead with his fingertips. "Can we meet around ten thirty? I should be able to have Silas ready to go by then."

"Perfect. See you tomorrow."

"Great. Thanks again." Sam slid behind the wheel of his rental SUV, put the directions to the resort into his phone, then started the engine. Before she turned and went inside her parents' house, Rylee waved. Sam backed out of the driveway slowly, then eased onto the road leading back toward town. He kept looking for Mr. and Mrs. Madden. By the time he got to the stop sign at the end of the road, he still hadn't passed them. He'd have to say thank-you another time.

On the short drive to the resort, he couldn't stop thinking about Rylee. The way her whole face lit up when she smiled. Her obvious love for her family. Her generosity. And as silly as he felt admitting it, he couldn't deny that he'd reacted when she'd innocently touched his hand.

How long had it been since he'd dated anyone?

At least two months. Maybe three. He'd dated a woman for several weeks in early spring, but she'd had no interest in anything other than her job at a prestigious Seattle law firm. They'd been set up on their first date by mutual friends and he'd had a great time. But as soon as she'd found out about his planned departure from his family's business, their relationship had fizzled out quickly. She hadn't liked to do anything outdoors, except attend professional baseball games. Sam suspected that she'd liked his season tickets and access to the Frazier family suite at the local stadium. He didn't miss her, but he'd also never intended to remain single well into his thirties.

After a short drive, he found the resort and slipped into a parking place. A romantic relationship would have to take a back seat now anyway. He had to stay focused on his reasons for visiting Hearts Bay. Celebrate Josh and Crystal's wedding and honor his commitment to his family's business by closing the deal and acquiring Hearts Bay Aviation. He'd meant what he'd said to Gus. This was his final opportunity to prove to his father that he cared about their family's stake in the industry. That leaving to pursue another career path didn't amount to a rejection of his father's values. Their sorrow over losing Lucas and Erin was still so raw that he hadn't found the appropriate time or the words to broach the conversation. Besides, actions meant more to his father.

He turned off the engine and pocketed the keys. Silas started to cry again. Sam exited the vehicle and opened the back door. With his small fist, Silas rubbed one of his eyes. His pitiful sound made Sam's chest tighten. He couldn't handle another sleepless night. Fumbling around in the car seat, he retrieved the pacifier and offered it again. Silas pushed out a quick breath, then took it.

Sam took out his phone to text Rylee and thank her again, then changed his mind. No need to go overboard on the gratitude. Her efforts to help with Silas had been far more accommodating than he'd expected. He wasn't confident she wanted anything to do with him, though. Besides, it was presumptuous to assume she was single. Her presence today had been a huge blessing, and he wouldn't turn away from her family's gracious assistance with Silas, but he couldn't start a relationship. Not now. His future plans and his new role as Silas's guardian took priority.

Chapter Three

"Wow, he's really cute." Chelsea, one of Crystal's bridesmaids, peered over Rylee's shoulder. "Who is he?"

"No one." Rylee closed out the app and flipped her phone facedown on her lap. Warmth blossomed on her skin. She avoided Chelsea's inquisitive gaze.

"Doesn't seem like no one." Chelsea leaned back on the maroon slip-covered love seat. "You had quite the smile on your face while you were looking at his picture."

Rylee shot her an irritated look. "I was not smiling."

Chelsea's pencil-thin eyebrows rose, but she said nothing. They were waiting in the spare room Crystal's parents had converted above their garage where Crystal's aunt Lisa, who had agreed to handle all the bridesmaids' dress alterations, would do their final fittings.

Rylee shoved her phone deep into her purse so she wouldn't be tempted to scroll again. At least not until Chelsea got up to change into her dress.

"How did you meet him? Wait. I heard about this." Chelsea clapped her hands together, her blue eyes gleaming. "The guy who showed up with a baby that no one knew about. Sean? Sam?"

"His name is Sam," Rylee said. "How'd you know about the baby?"

"Because my brother was on the same flight as him from Anchorage. He said the baby cried the whole way here."

Rylee winced. Sam had told her the same thing. Poor Silas. The little guy did cry quite a bit. But who could blame him?

"Sam is Josh's best man. They've been friends since college." Rylee took an elastic band from around her wrist and twisted her hair into a loose ponytail. "The baby is his nephew."

"So why are you looking at his picture?"

"Okay, ladies." Lisa returned from the restroom. In her midfifties, she wore a red-and-white-striped T-shirt and denim shorts. She'd twisted her long black hair into a single braid and she had a fabric tape measure draped around her neck. "Who's up next?"

"I'll go." Rylee stood and lifted the blue

chiffon skirt as she walked barefoot across the beige-and-cream shag carpet. The extra room had served numerous purposes over the years. A guest room for out-of-town relatives, a gaming area for Crystal's brothers, and now a temporary fitting room for the wedding party.

"Stand here, please." Lisa pointed to the plywood box Crystal's father had built for the occasion.

Rylee stepped up onto the platform, faced the mirror and studied her reflection. She didn't dress up often. Okay, hardly ever. Thankfully, Crystal had chosen bridesmaids' dresses in a flattering color. The sweetheart neckline, fitted bodice and short puffed sleeves were a little too feminine for Rylee's tastes, but she wasn't going to complain.

"All right, hold still." Lisa removed the measuring tape from around her neck and examined the dress's hem. "We need to take a smidge off the bottom here. Did you bring your shoes?"

"Oh, right." Rylee glanced back over her shoulder. "Chelsea, can you bring me that shoebox, please? It's on the floor next to your bag."

Chelsea grinned but didn't move from her spot on the love seat. "If you'll tell me that guy's last name. I want to look at his social media."

Rylee groaned. "Really?"

Chelsea shrugged. "Why not? Like I said, he's a cutie."

"I thought you were seeing someone."

"I am, but we've only been on three dates. Nothing serious."

"Bring me the shoes, please," Rylee said.

Chelsea didn't move. "What's Sam's last name?"

"Bring me the shoes and I'll tell you."

Chelsea quirked her lips to one side.

Lisa met Rylee's gaze in the mirror. "I have four more fittings after this, girls. No rush or anything."

Rylee blew out a long breath. "Fi-iine. His last name is Frazier. Now bring me my shoes."

"Frazier. Got it." Chelsea jumped up, snagged the silver open-toed sandals from the box and carried them over. "Here you go."

"Thanks." Rylee slipped them on and then straightened to her full height.

Honestly, what had she been thinking? Searching for Sam on social media with Chelsea sitting right beside her? Not that she'd admit this to anyone, but curiosity had gotten the best of her. She'd wanted to know more about this man who had arrived in Hearts Bay after enduring the loss of his brother and sister-in-law and then assuming responsibility for an infant. Crystal didn't know much about him, and Rylee hadn't had time to ask Josh any questions. That wasn't a smart choice, anyway. Josh would surely tell Sam she'd asked about him and then where would she be?

"I found him." Chelsea glanced up from her phone. "He must love the outdoors. Most of his feed is pictures of him hiking or on a boat at a lake. When are you going to see him again?"

A pang of jealousy squeezed Rylee's insides. Why did she care if Chelsea looked at Sam's social media? Rylee wasn't interested. Okay, maybe a little interested. But they'd only just met. She shifted from one foot to the other, eager to be finished.

"Hold still, honey," Lisa said. "I need to get these measurements right or you'll have a crooked hem."

"Sorry."

"Chelsea, you can go ahead and get changed into your dress," Lisa said. "I'll be ready for you in a few minutes."

"All right. But after I change, I want to know—what's the story behind the baby?" Chelsea stood and walked toward the bathroom with her dress draped over her arm. "And I need to know if Sam is single."

Rylee didn't answer. Chelsea shot her another look before she closed the bathroom door.

Lisa removed a straight pin from the cushion

she'd balanced on a stack of shoeboxes nearby. "Maybe if we distract her with trying on her dress, she'll ease up on the questions."

Rylee offered a grateful smile. "Thank you."

"No problem."

While Lisa finished pinning the hem, Rylee's thoughts returned to Sam. She was scheduled to give him a tour of the island today. An intriguing fact she definitely would not be sharing with Chelsea. The girl would spread that news all over Hearts Bay before Rylee and Sam even drove out of the resort's parking lot. She also had the name and contact info for a friend of Tess's who was interested in babysitting Silas. Not quite the same as a full-time nanny but it was a good start in finding dependable childcare for the next three weeks. Or however long Sam and Silas stayed on the island. Rylee planned to reassure Sam she'd help him with Silas whenever she could. He'd clearly been anxious about making sure his nephew had what he needed. That poor baby. He'd endured so much already.

"How are the Suttons doing?" Lisa asked. "I've seen their daughter's name on the church prayer request list for several weeks in a row."

"Paul's pretending that everything is fine," Rylee said softly. "But I think he's having a tough time. Libby really wants to move to Nevada. She'd be gone already if it were up to her. Their daughter is a single mom with four kids and needs help. That's why they're selling the business."

With Chelsea right on the other side of the closed bathroom door, Rylee refused to tell Lisa that Sam was here on behalf of Frazier Aviation in addition to being best man. The Sutton family could share the news in their own time about who had bought Hearts Bay Aviation. They hadn't signed any papers yet. The deal could still fall through. Besides, if she told Lisa, then that might trigger the inevitable question of how the acquisition impacted Rylee's job. Sure, there were plenty of other places in Alaska where she could work as a pilot, but she wanted to stay in Hearts Bay. This was her home.

"Dad, we're doing fine. There's no need for you and Mom to worry."

There were actually plenty of reasons to worry, but Sam wasn't about to add anything else to his father's list of heartbreaking circumstances to mull over. They'd already lost a son, a daughter-in-law, and now Sam had whisked their only grandchild off to Alaska. Why was he surprised that Dad had called already to check in?

"I'm concerned about you, son. A baby and

an acquisition are a lot for you to tackle, even for someone like yourself who's accustomed to being a high achiever."

Sam stood in his suite at the resort, keeping a close eye on Silas lying on a bath towel Sam had spread on the carpeted floor. Thanks to a recent diaper-related disaster, Sam had just finished cleaning the boy up and wrangling him into a new diaper when Dad had called.

Was it okay for a baby to lie around in just a diaper? Silas seemed happy, cooing at the ceiling and holding on to his bare toes. He pulled his knees up to his stomach a lot. Was that normal? Sam made a mental note to research that online later.

"Silas and I are taking life one day at a time," Sam said, crossing to the closet where he'd shoved one of the duffel bags last night.

"I wish you would've taken full-time help along with you," Dad said. "Your mother and I would feel better knowing that you had some assistance."

Sam bit back a comment about how they could've come along if they'd wanted to. Or Sam could've stayed back in Seattle with Silas and let his father handle the acquisition. That wasn't kind. Or even necessary. Because he was here and his parents weren't. No point in getting into a debate now. He also had the wedding.

"I'm working on finding reliable childcare." He dug around in the bag for clean baby clothes. At the rate Silas was going messing up his pajamas, Sam would need to figure out how to do laundry soon. "How are you and mom doing?"

Dad sighed. "We're getting by. Still waiting to hear from Erin's family about plans for a memorial service. Erin's brother lives overseas, so it's an ordeal trying to coordinate schedules."

"I understand." Sam chose a white onesie and a green one-piece outfit with a zipper from the bottom of the leg to the collar. Perfect. Because if he had to snap all those snaps together like he had on the pajamas Silas wore yesterday, they'd be here until lunch.

"We'd rather not wait until August to have a service, but we're trying to respect Erin's family's preferences. One memorial service will be easier on all of us," Dad said.

Sam swallowed hard. He couldn't believe they were even discussing a memorial service. Lucas's and Erin's deaths still didn't seem real. He hated that working through these details had created tension between the two families, but Sam couldn't worry about that now. Eventually, they would come to agree on the time and location. His job was to keep Silas safe and well cared for. The wedding and acquisition came next on his to-do list.

"Listen, Dad, I'd love to keep chatting but I've got to figure out how to feed Silas and get him dressed and ready for my first meeting."

"Which meeting is that?"

"Thanks again for checking in. Give Mom my love and I'll be in touch." He ended the call before his father could protest. If the senior leadership team at Frazier wanted him to handle this, then they needed to let him do his job. Dad had probably never interfered with Lucas's day-to-day operations. He shoved that thought right back where it came from. He was way too deep in the trenches of grief to start making senseless comparisons.

Instead, he shifted his focus to Rylee and the way she'd smiled and held Silas like he was precious cargo. Despite his silent proclamations in the car last night that he didn't have space in his life for a relationship, he was still looking forward to seeing her soon. He glanced at the alarm clock on his bedside table. Very soon. Yikes. He'd agreed to meet her in less than twenty minutes and Silas wasn't dressed yet. Sam had improved his technique at maneuvering a squirmy baby into his clothes but it still took him far longer than he felt was reasonable.

Silas started to fuss.

"One second, my man." Sam opened his text messages and quickly reviewed the itinerary that Rylee had sent him. "I need to make sure we've dressed appropriately for today's adventures."

She'd planned lunch at a local restaurant called The Tide Pool, followed by a tour of a new housing development, then a quick meeting with staff at the airport. That might be too much for Silas. They'd have to reschedule the meeting because the little fella would need a nap this afternoon. Preferably a long one.

An unpleasant sound pulled Sam's attention from his phone. "Silas? Are you all right?"

A putrid smell filled the room. What in the world? Sam grabbed the collar of his sweatshirt and pulled it up over his nose. He tossed his phone on the bed and turned in time to see Silas's sweet little face crumple. His now-familiar wail echoed off the walls of the hotel room.

Sam tentatively approached then sank to his knees beside his nephew lying on the soiled towel. "Oh, buddy. Baby wipes are not going to salvage this."

Silas cried louder. His hands were squeezed into tight little fists and he pulled his knees up to his belly.

Sam reluctantly let go of his sweatshirt. Gagging, he forced himself to press his palm against Silas's abdomen. A splotchy red rash dotted the baby's skin.

"Man, you are having a tough time. Don't worry. I'm here and we're going to figure this out together."

Except he had no idea how. Was he supposed to contact the front desk? Housekeeping? A baby's mess wasn't their responsibility, though. He could probably take care of bathing Silas on his own, and sending the clothes out to be laundered, but he had to figure out why the boy kept getting so sick. This couldn't be normal.

As much as he wanted to bravely handle this, it was time to call for backup. He scooped Silas into his arms, keeping the towel wrapped around him. He stood and retrieved his phone from the bed. With a grouchy Silas tucked against him, Sam managed to peck out a text message for Rylee.

Good morning. I'm so sorry to ask you to do this but could you come to our suite and help me out? Silas is a mess and I'm not sure what to do.

After he hit Send, he awkwardly bounced up and down the same way he'd seen other people do with crying infants. Silas's cries matched the rhythm of Sam's movement. Sam stared at the phone.

"Please, please check your messages," he whispered. Silas cried louder and arched his back, getting angrier by the minute. "I know, I know."

Sam crossed the room to the window. As if a gorgeous view of Hearts Bay would soothe a miserable infant. "I'm asking one of our new friends to come and help. I promise we're going to get you squared away."

Silas twisted in Sam's arms and stared up at him. His face had turned redder and the strange rash from his stomach appeared to be spreading across his chest. A rash, excessive crying, stomach issues…as soon as he heard from Rylee and had Silas bathed and dressed, he'd look all of that up. His tour of Hearts Bay would have to wait.

The dots on the screen bounced, stopped, and bounced again. Finally, Rylee's response popped up on the screen.

I'll be right there. What's the room number?

"Oh, thank you, Lord." He offered the prayer heavenward, then sent her a quick response with his room number. A package of baby wipes sat on the desk. He grabbed it, hesitated, and put it back. Was there something in the wipes irritating Silas's skin? That didn't seem logical. Then again, he was a numbers guy. Woefully inadequate and ill-prepared to navigate parenthood.

Why had he been entrusted with a helpless infant? Had Lucas and Erin known something was wrong with Silas before they'd left? Why hadn't they mentioned it? The questions piled up as Sam paced the room with a distraught Silas in his arms. Regret made his stomach churn. He never should've come to Hearts Bay.

Rylee's heart hammered as she strode from the elevator down the corridor toward Sam and Silas's suite at the resort. His text message sounded so urgent. Maybe even a little desperate.

Rylee stopped outside room 308 and knocked softly. The dead bolt turned and Sam opened the door. He held Silas in his arms, wrapped in a white bath towel. Silas fussed and reached for her. Oh, what a sweet baby. An unpleasant smell wafted from the room.

"Thanks for coming." Sam's forehead creased with concern. "Sorry about the stench."

She tried to pretend she hadn't noticed. "Rough morning?"

"Extremely." Sam stepped back and held the door open with his body. "I hate to bring you into this disaster, but will you please help me?"

Silas screeched louder and kicked his legs against Sam's torso as he stretched both of his little arms toward Rylee.

"Hi, pumpkin. Come here." Rylee stepped into the room and tried to lift Silas from Sam's arms.

Sam hesitated. "Are you sure? He's filthy."

"I'll keep him wrapped in the towel until we figure out what to do. Did you bring an infant bathtub?"

Sam shook his head. "I wish. That's one of the few baby-related items I left behind. Too bulky."

"True." Rylee stepped inside the bathroom and looked around. "We can make do with what we have. My grandmother bathed me in the kitchen sink all the time."

"Really? I didn't know that was safe." Sam dragged his hand over his face. "But I don't have a better suggestion, and we've got to do something to get him cleaned up."

Silas shoved a finger in the side of his mouth and stared at Sam. Rylee surveyed the modern bathroom. White fluffy towels were stacked on the shelf under the sink. A black travel-size hairdryer sat next to a leather bag with a zipper and Sam's initials on the outside.

"Do you have his baby soap and shampoo?" She gently bounced Silas up and down in her arms. He caught their reflection in the mirror and grinned.

"You must be feeling a little better if you're smiling." Rylee pressed a quick kiss to his forehead. The weight of Sam's stare caught her attention. Oh, no.

"I'm sorry, was that too forward? I haven't earned the right to kiss your nephew's head yet, have I?"

Sam's Adam's apple bobbed up and down as he swallowed hard. "No, it was, uh, just really sweet, that's all."

She whirled away, spotting the baby shampoo and soap on the edge of the bathtub. "Found what I need. I'll run some warm water and get him all cleaned up."

After propping the suite's door open with a suitcase, Sam leaned against the bathroom doorframe. Rylee appreciated Sam's sense of propriety. "Here's the thing. He's got this weird rash and he's been dealing with a lot of upset stomach issues."

"And he cries a lot," Rylee added. She turned on the sink spigot and adjusted the temperature. "Have you called your pediatrician?"

"I don't even know his pediatrician. Erin, his mom, was a heart surgeon. She had planned on going back to work next week. Since she's been home for six months with him, she handled all those arrangements. I probably have it written down somewhere in the notes she left with my folks. They watched Silas before I took over."

"Okay, one thing at a time." She gently

braced Silas on the counter, still keeping the towel wrapped around him. Carefully plucking her phone from her back pocket, she set it out of Silas's reach and scrolled to Mia's contact information. "How about if I text Mia? She's Gus's wife and works as a physician assistant. Maybe she can give us some advice."

"Great plan," Sam said. "Thank you."

Rylee tapped out a quick message to Mia, explaining the situation, then hit Send and handed her phone to Sam. "I'll tell you what. Why don't you hang on to this in case she responds and I'll focus on cleaning up this sweet boy."

Sam nodded and took the phone. "Perfect. I'll be right out here if you need me."

Rylee bit back a laugh.

"Wait." Sam held up his hand. "Forget I said that. Obviously, I am way out of my element here and need all the help I can get. And I appreciate it."

"No worries."

Silas leaned forward and tried to touch the water pouring from the sink spigot.

"Oh, not so fast, clever man. Let's double-check the water temperature so it's just right for you."

Silas shrieked and smacked his palm against the mirror.

Rylee cringed. She'd never actually bathed a baby before, but how hard could it be?

Fifteen minutes later, sweaty and exasperated, she'd dropped the last clean dry towel in the bathroom on the floor and managed to get a slippery wet Silas safely out of the sink.

Sam popped his head into the bathroom. "How's it going in here?"

"Remind me not to do that ever again."

Sam chuckled. "Not a fan of bathroom sink baths?"

She gently toweled water droplets off Silas's face. He squealed and kicked his legs. "This seemed like such a good idea. I remember having a ball when my grandmother put me in the sink."

"You must have been quite a bit older than Silas if you can remember that."

"Yeah, you're probably right. I thought it would be easier. Or at least safer. Did Mia respond yet?"

"Yes. Hope you don't mind but I read the message. She said she's coming here."

"That's great." Rylee offered him a hopeful smile. "She's amazing. I'm glad she's stopping by because this rash on Silas's tummy is gnarly."

"I know." Sam dragged his hand over his face. "I'm worried."

"Hello?" Mia's voice filtered in from the hallway.

Sam pushed away from the bathroom door and motioned for her to join them. "Come on in. I'm Sam. Thank you so much for stopping by."

"Hey, Sam. It's nice to meet you. I'm sorry I couldn't join you for dinner last night." Mia peeked into the bathroom. Her auburn waves were twisted into a bun, and she wore a green V-necked T-shirt, jeans, and canvas sneakers. "Hi, Rylee. How's he doing?"

Rylee sat back on her heels. "You're just in time. We got this little guy all cleaned up."

"Oh, he's a cutie pie." Mia smiled and held up her leather bag. "I brought my not-so-secret weapons. Sam, if you don't mind, I'd like to examine Silas. How about if we put him on the bed?"

"Of course." Sam gestured for her to lead the way.

Rylee finished drying Silas off and put him in the clean diaper that Sam had brought her. She picked Silas up, cradled him close, and joined Mia and Sam in the spacious hotel room.

"I think he's mostly dry." She carefully set him in the middle of the bed.

Silas started to cry, his little hands forming fists, and he bicycled his legs in the air.

"He does that a lot." Sam's brow furrowed. "Does it mean anything?"

"Maybe." Mia breathed on the round part of her stethoscope. "Let me warm this up and I'll listen to his heart and lungs. I see the rash on his torso. Hopefully, I'll have some answers for you in a few minutes."

Rylee stepped back and chewed on her thumbnail. Silas kept crying and tried to twist away from Mia as she performed a quick examination. Rylee stole a glance at Sam. He looked so stressed that her fingers itched to reach out and squeeze his arm. What in the world? They'd only just met. She had no right to comfort him. Tamping down the thought, she watched as Mia listened to Silas's heart and lungs, peeked inside his ears and his nose, then gently ran her fingertips across the rash on his tummy.

"When did you first notice this?"

Sam lifted one shoulder. "This morning."

"Have you changed the formula he's drinking?"

Sam sighed. "That's the one thing in his life that hasn't changed lately. His parents passed away unexpectedly, and I've been feeding him the formula that they left for him."

Mia glanced up, her green eyes filled with empathy. "I'm so sorry for your loss."

"Thank you," Sam said. "At first I thought he

cried all the time because he didn't know me and he wanted his mom and dad. But it's been over a week. He throws up frequently and has had more diarrhea than one infant should have."

Mia nodded and turned her attention back to Silas. "So, without running any blood work or knowing anything about his health history, my hunch is he might be allergic to something in the formula."

Sam's face fell. "Allergic? Are you saying everything I've fed him makes him sick?"

Rylee's breath hitched. Poor guy. This time she didn't hesitate to reach over and squeeze his arm. "This is not your fault. We're going to help you figure out what Silas needs."

Sam blanketed her hand with his own. Their eyes locked. She couldn't look away. This wasn't wise, what she was doing. Getting involved in Sam's life. Helping him resolve his personal crisis. In a matter of weeks, she might be out of a job if his company acquired Hearts Bay Aviation. But she'd just have to come up with creative methods to fortify her heart because she certainly wasn't going to turn her back on a sweet baby and his overwhelmed uncle.

Chapter Four

"I can't believe that baby food and formula got here so quickly." Sam slid the box of infant formula into the back of his rental, next to the variety pack of pureed baby food, then closed the hatch. The pungent aroma of diesel fuel wafted toward him as a truck eased to the curb outside the airport's entrance and dropped off a passenger.

"We take a request for a rush delivery quite seriously." Rylee's keys jangled as she pulled them from the pocket of her raincoat. "Especially when someone is in desperate need."

"Well, I was certainly desperate." Sam faced her. "I can't thank you enough. After Silas drank that sample of the new formula Mia gave us at the clinic yesterday, he was like a different baby. So happy, and we both slept well."

"That's a blessing when a fussy baby finally

falls asleep." Rylee tipped her head to one side. The silvery gray beads on her dangly earrings swayed as she studied him. "I'm thrilled that Mia was able to help."

"It wasn't just Mia. Your family has been so gracious. I'm blown away." Sam pulled his phone from his pocket. He'd become even more conscious of time and maintaining a schedule since he'd become Silas's guardian. "Can I take you to lunch? A meal will never be enough to make up for all you've done, but it's a start."

Rylee waved him off. "Don't worry about it. My family really cannot stand by and do nothing when they see someone knee-deep in a crisis."

"So I shouldn't think of myself as special? Is that what you're saying?"

Her pink lips curved into a smile and her beautiful eyes lit up. Oh, wow. His pulse sped. She was stunning.

"Um, that's not what I said," she teased. "What I meant was we help each other out. It's a way of life on the island. And even though you are considered a VIP around here, we would have helped you and Silas no matter what."

He chuckled, then dipped his head, pushing a pebble away with the toe of his hiking boot. What was going on? Were they flirting? That was hardly professional. He wasn't in Hearts

Bay because he needed a girlfriend. Besides, she'd only done her job. Flown to Anchorage and back this morning to pick up his rush order of baby food and special formula for Silas. Now he was standing there like a goofball. Trying to get her to have lunch with him.

His phone hummed. "Excuse me. I'd better check this."

He'd never been one to ignore a call or a text, but he'd become especially more attentive when Silas was with a babysitter. After he read the message, he met Rylee's curious gaze.

"This is from your mom. She says Silas just went down for a nap and he's sleeping soundly. Not to worry."

"You definitely don't need to worry. My mother is fantastic with kids and babies. She's probably working the phones trying to find you a full-time sitter. Have you decided how long you're staying?"

"We're leaving on the eighteenth. Four days after the wedding." The sharp whir of a twin-propeller plane taking off kept Sam from saying more. Rylee tipped her head back, her silky dark ponytail bobbing, as she used her hand to shield her eyes from the afternoon sunlight.

A persistent rain had doused Hearts Bay all morning, but then the weather had improved shortly before Rylee had landed with her freight. The gray clouds that had greeted Sam when he woke this morning had since parted. Now the puddles on the airport parking lot's asphalt reflected the lush green mountains that edged the runway.

"So, what do you say? Can I take you to lunch?"

Rylee hesitated, then checked her phone. "I have about four hours before I'm scheduled for an evening flightseeing tour."

"Oh, I didn't realize that was a service your company provided," Sam said, making a mental note to revisit the files waiting on his hard drive. He'd spent so much time coping with his brother's and sister-in-law's deaths and trying to meet Silas's needs that he hadn't had much time to focus on the acquisition.

Rylee's brows knitted together. "How much do you know about Hearts Bay Aviation?"

"Not as much as I would like."

"Then we probably should have lunch," Rylee said. "I'll bring you up to speed."

"Great." Sam tried not to dwell on the fact that she'd just turned this into a business meeting rather than an opportunity for him to thank her for helping him out.

"I'll text you the address for The Tide Pool." Rylee's fingers danced over her device. "It's a local favorite and a great place for a quick lunch."

"Sounds perfect."

A few seconds later, his phone hummed again. "Message received. I'll see you there."

"See you soon." Rylee pocketed her phone and strode toward her vehicle.

Sam slid behind the wheel of his rental. He set up his phone to sync with the vehicle, then prompted the navigation system to get him to the correct restaurant. Orca Island didn't seem large enough for him to get lost, but he'd been so concerned about Silas that he had paid very little attention to his surroundings since he'd been here. After he buckled his seat belt, he slowly headed out of the parking lot.

As he drove, he lowered the window and let the cool tangy air wash into the car. The modest homes with well-kept lawns, planters overflowing with blooming flowers, and glimpses of trampolines and play structures underscored his initial assessment of Hearts Bay. People here cared about each other and loved their families. Sam slowed his vehicle to a stop at a crosswalk and waited while a young family strolled in front of him, with a handsome Goldendoodle on a leash walking beside them.

This really was a gorgeous community. Quite the opposite of the sophisticated upscale lifestyle he'd grown accustomed to in Seattle. There was something refreshing about a rugged island in the middle of the ocean. The way people pulled together to solve a problem, opened their homes to strangers, and made sure that a baby they'd never met received fantastic medical care. He still couldn't get over the fact that Mia had stopped by the resort and calmly assessed Silas. Then she'd asked Sam to bring Silas to the clinic where she worked for further evaluation. It had been a stressful day yesterday, but by evening, Mia had diagnosed Silas's intolerance to formula and established a plan.

Thank You, Lord, for caring for us, keeping us safe, and surrounding us with kind and caring people, especially when we're so far from home.

Guilt rushed in, squelching his gratitude. Man, he'd been foolish, thinking he could bring Silas here and take care of him alone. Sure, the Maddens had come to his rescue, but now what was he going to do? He'd never fed a baby anything besides a bottle, and he wasn't all that good at that. Starting Silas on his new formula, and rice cereal plus solid food felt like another insurmountable challenge.

The dog barked, his tail wagging, pulling Sam from his thoughts. Since the family had safely crossed to the opposite sidewalk with their pet and their stroller, Sam eased down on the accelerator.

He could do this. He could be the guardian

that Silas needed and oversee this acquisition. He just had to regroup. Stay focused on what mattered—keeping Silas safe and healthy and acquiring Hearts Bay Aviation. Oh, and being the best man at Josh and Crystal's wedding. Sam groaned and gripped the steering wheel tighter. Maybe he had overcommitted. Since he'd arrived on the island, he'd slid further and further outside his comfort zone.

This was so not a good idea.

Rylee eased her car into one of the few open parking spaces outside The Tide Pool. Great. The place was packed. Why hadn't she paid attention to her gut instinct and declined Sam's invitation? Once again, her leap-first-and-reflect-on-her-choices-later approach to life had landed her in a tight spot. They really shouldn't be having lunch together. Carson or Libby or one of the other seasoned pilots could tell Sam everything he needed to know about owning a business on Orca Island. Sam had flown to the island for two reasons. Acquire Hearts Bay Aviation and be the best man in their mutual friend's wedding. Crystal's matchmaking comments resurfaced. Like an overstuffed carry-on bag on a crowded flight, Rylee shoved those thoughts into the mental space where she tucked things she didn't want to think about.

Except Sam had been having a tough time since he and Silas had arrived. And just like the rest of her family, she didn't have the heart to turn away when someone was obviously struggling. Maybe it wasn't too late to suggest a different place to eat, though. After a lifetime in this close-knit community, she could already envision the curious stares that would follow them as they made their way to their table inside the restaurant.

In her rearview mirror, she spotted Sam in his SUV, pulling into the parking lot.

"We'll talk about aviation. Bridal party responsibilities. Josh and Crystal's meet-cute," she said, turning off the ignition. Okay, maybe not that last part. Sam didn't seem like the kind of guy who was into chatting about meet-cutes.

She grabbed her purse and climbed out of the car. Sam unfolded his tall frame, stood and stretched, then grinned at her over the roof of his vehicle. Her heart shot skyward, then dropped into a tailslide like an airplane performing a high-risk aerobatic maneuver.

Oh, no, you don't. She promptly admonished her fickle heart. Still, she returned his smile. There was no need to be rude. Besides, it wasn't like he'd asked to be plunked into this scenario. And he was handsome. Especially with those lines that crinkled around the corners of his eyes when he smiled. That shock of dark hair he tried to tame into submission. His broad shoulders and athletic build would definitely draw some approving glances.

"How long has this place been around?" Sam scanned the sign displayed high on a pole in the middle of the parking lot, promoting their current special.

"As long as I can remember. It's owned by a local family, and you really can't go wrong with anything you order." Rylee swung her purse strap over her shoulder. "Fish and chips, cheeseburgers or clam chowder are all excellent. If you're a vegetarian, they have a really good black bean burger."

"I'm not a vegetarian," Sam said, gravel crunching under his sneakers as they walked toward the entrance. "I appreciate the suggestions."

She ducked her chin. Wow, she'd started to babble. Why was she so nervous?

Sam opened the door wide and held it for her so she could walk through first. Every single person seated at the six tables closest to the door turned and stared. Rylee's legs itched to scoot right back out the door. Why did she care so much what people thought? This wasn't a date. She forced herself to move toward the hostess stand.

"Hey, Rylee." Her friend Abby collected menus and utensils wrapped in white paper napkins. "Two for lunch?"

Rylee nodded, suddenly unable to form words. Sam stepped closer to accommodate a party of four exiting the restaurant. His shoulder accidentally brushed against hers. Could her face get any hotter?

"Right this way." Abby led them to a high top with four stools near the window. "You'll find more information about our specials on the card inside the menu."

Sam flashed her a polite smile. "Thank you."

After placing the menus in front of them, Abby hovered beside the table. Rylee shrugged out of her jacket and pretended not to notice the curiosity swimming in her friend's eyes. "It's good to see you, Abby."

She didn't owe Abby an introduction to Sam. Did she?

"Enjoy your meal," Abby said, discreetly mouthing *Text me everything* before returning to her post near the door.

Not happening. Because there wasn't anything to text about. He'd invited her to lunch to thank her for helping him and Silas navigate a medical issue. She'd only said yes because he'd clearly needed more details regarding the acquisition.

Strictly professional.

Sam politely waited for her to sit down first. She chose the stool that kept her back to the window. Facing the inside of the restaurant granted Sam the best seat with an amazing view of the harbor. That was the right thing to do. He'd probably feel more comfortable if he didn't notice how often people glanced their way.

He took off his jacket and draped it over the vacant stool beside his, then sat across from her. "This is a nice place. It has a great vibe."

"My family have been customers here for years. There are other good restaurants on the island, but this is probably our favorite." Rylee found the hook under the table for her purse, then reached for the laminated menu. Not that she didn't already have the thing memorized. The Tide Pool had given the place a mini make-over recently and added a few new options. She had tried a few of the entrées, including the chef's salad. But today, she craved her usual. Clam chowder in a sourdough bread bowl and a basic side salad.

After the server came and took their orders for drinks and their lunch, including an order of The Tide Pool's legendary pretzel bites appetizer, a comfortable silence blanketed their table. Too comfortable, to be honest. She couldn't let this lunch meeting slide into dangerous territory. The kind of territory where they didn't talk shop at all. She had to follow through on her commitment to bring him up to speed.

"So." She rubbed her palms together. "Let me tell you everything I know about owning a small business in Hearts Bay. Are you ready?"

Sam nodded and shifted his weight on his stool. Two divots appeared between his brows.

Rylee hesitated. "You look a little uncertain."

His gaze lifted and he smiled, but something she couldn't quite decipher lingered in his eyes. "I'm ready. Let me grab my phone and take some notes."

The server returned with their sodas and Rylee waited until he retrieved the device from his pocket.

"All right. Bring it."

"Paul and Libby have been in business since they graduated from college. Paul's probably been flying for most of his life. Libby has run the front office. She knows everything there is to know about the business. You should really connect with her as soon as you can." Rylee unwrapped a straw and popped it into her drink. "We have eight aircraft in the fleet, which is a lot, given the cost of fuel, maintenance needs and hours we put in."

Sam paused his note-taking. "How many pilots on staff and are you all full-time?"

"Five full-time pilots and one who has asked to cut back to twenty hours so he can spend more time with his kids this summer. We divide our time between transport and tourism. For example, this morning's run to Anchorage for formula and insulin. Also, we pick up more tourism and private parties whenever we can. Those are more lucrative."

"What does a private party flight consist of?"

"Depends on the demand. During the summer, we fly groups out to the fishing lodges and we do a lot of short flights over the bay and around the island. That sort of thing."

"What about medical emergencies?"

"Most of those are handled by the Coast Guard. They have a significant presence here, with a base and an air station. But, of course, if somebody needs transport, we don't ever say no. If the weather's decent and we have fuel for the plane, we go."

"How about animals? Is there a veterinarian here on the island?"

"There's a small practice with two veterinarians. I've flown quite a few animals over to the Kenai Peninsula for more complicated treatments." She reached for her soda. "You're asking great questions, Sam."

"I'm trying." His fingers danced over the keyboard on his phone.

She opened her mouth to delve deeper, but there was something about his expression that puzzled her. "Is this interesting to you?"

His head shot up. "Yeah, of course. Aviation is why I'm here. I mean one of the reasons why."

"You'd mentioned to Gus that you're into making sure people have clean water. So I'm wondering if this acquisition is really your thing."

His mouth tightened. And she instantly wished she could snatch the words back. "I'm sorry. I shouldn't have—"

"No." He set his phone facedown and fiddled with the paper ring encircling his napkin-wrapped silverware. "You nailed it. Actually, I'm… This is not my passion. I'm just trying to be a good son and keep my word. Especially with everything my family is going through right now."

"That's very kind of you," she said softly.

"And I wanted to be here for Josh and Crystal. He's been a good friend to me over the years. It's important to celebrate their big day."

"Absolutely."

The server returned with two small plates, extra napkins and a basket of pretzel bites. Even though they hadn't spent much time together, Sam's loyalty to his family and his passion for making the world a better place was quite obvious. Still, she couldn't let his admirable qualities blind her to the truth. This acquisition could lead to unemployment.

She added cheese sauce to her plate along with a few pretzel bites, then passed the basket to Sam. "Enjoy."

"Thank you." His generous smile and the warmth of his fingers brushing against hers sent a delightful zing up her arm.

She quickly averted her gaze. Yeah, okay, so he was kind, and fun to hang out with. And that smile could really make her go all wobbly in the knees if she wasn't careful. But there was no doubt in her mind that he'd honor his commitment to his family, even though he planned to leave the aviation industry to pursue other opportunities. If that meant restructuring, or bringing in trusted staff from Seattle, Sam wouldn't let their friendship influence his business decisions. So she'd have to work extra hard to prove that she deserved to stay on as one of the company's most reliable pilots.

Sam blew on the top of the steaming cup of coffee he'd just brewed from the single-cup appliance on the counter in his suite. It had been a long and busy day. But now that Silas had the right formula and had happily eaten an entire container of pureed pears, Sam hoped the little guy might sleep for several hours tonight. Because Sam had more than enough work to keep him busy into the wee hours.

He walked carefully across the carpet toward the desk that now served as his temporary workstation. Before he sat down, he checked the video baby monitor perched on the dresser, even though Silas's portable crib was probably less than twenty feet away in the other bedroom. He'd be able to work more efficiently if he could see with his own eyes that all was well.

Silas had fallen asleep with both arms stretched above his head. Sam smiled. The tension camped in the muscles between his shoulder blades lessened a little at the adorable sight. He had a white noise app playing peaceful raindrops, the door tightly closed and the blackout shades drawn to block out the daylight. It was after 9:00 p.m. but summer was still going strong outside the resort. Somewhere music played and occasionally muffled conversation echoed in the hall as guests passed by his door.

He'd held his breath the whole time the coffeemaker was chugging and hissing, dispensing his much-needed caffeine. What if his selfish craving woke up the baby? Sam should probably try to get some sleep just in case they were up in the middle of the night together. But the spreadsheets on his computer monitor and the stack of files on the desk reminded him that he didn't have the luxury of going to bed early. Paul and Libby were returning to the island tomorrow. Sam wasn't even close to prepared for their first meeting. Sighing, he lowered the coffee mug to his desk and sat in the padded chair. He was not the guy for this acquisition. That had become painfully obvious during his lunch with Rylee today. They hadn't delved into the topic deeply but he'd still sat there in awe of her knowledge about the industry and the grit and determination it took to run a small company on an island.

Sam's phone hummed with an incoming text. He picked it up and glanced at the screen. A message from Josh. Oh, yeah, the groom. The guy Sam was supposed to be the best man for. He raked his hand through his hair. Another thing he was falling ridiculously behind on— being a decent friend during one of the most significant events of Josh's life.

Hey, just checking in. Can't believe we haven't seen each other yet. There's a lunch tomorrow at a local park. We're celebrating Crystal's birthday, then a few of us are going fishing. Nothing too intense. Let me know if you want to come along. I'll make sure there's a pole and plenty of bait.

Sam stared at the screen. He could barely keep Silas in clean clothes and dry diapers. The first feeding tonight had taken forever. And made a big mess. What in the world would he do with a baby if he tried to go fishing?

Guilt swept in as he thought about declining Josh's offer. They had to hang out sometime. Sam scanned the message again. Depending on the timing and the weather, he could probably handle lunch in the park. Somewhere in his mountain of baby equipment he'd spotted a portable high chair for Silas. He typed out a quick response.

Yes to lunch. Sounds great. Send me the address and I'll try to be there. I'll have to pass on fishing. Silas isn't quite ready to learn how to cast the line. But thanks for thinking of us.

He sent the message. Regret immediately knifed at him. Had he told Josh about Silas?

Surely he had. But the days following his brother's and Erin's deaths had been a blur. He couldn't be sure he'd followed through on letting Josh know his plus-one was a six-month-old.

Three dots bounced on the screen. Josh's response arrived with a whoosh.

We could probably help you find a babysitter for Silas if you want to go fishing.

Nope. The Maddens had given him a short list of local folks to contact about babysitting. He'd planned to tackle those calls tomorrow during Silas's naps.

Thanks, but I'm being super cautious about whom I leave him with right now. Rylee is helping me line somebody up for the rehearsal dinner and the wedding. Don't sweat. I know Crystal would rather I not bring a baby to your wedding.

The three dots bounced again then stopped. Then bounced and stopped. Sam set the phone down and reached for his coffee.

I'm hanging out with my brother and my dad here at the house if you want to come by. We'll probably be here for a few more hours.

Irritation flared. Did Josh read anything Sam had just sent him?

Thanks but I'll have to pass. Silas is already asleep.

Josh sent back a palm-to-forehead emoji along with an apology.

Sorry man. Didn't think about that. I'm still living a kid-free life. Catch you later.

Sam put his phone down without responding. Josh hadn't meant to be thoughtless. The guy likely had a lot on his mind. Besides, it wasn't Josh's fault that Sam's family had experienced a senseless tragedy. Or chosen to acquire Hearts Bay Aviation. Or that his parents were so distraught that they could barely function.

He scrubbed his palm across his face and stared at the ceiling. He had to find a way to balance parenthood, his responsibilities with Frazier Aviation, and his commitment to being Josh's best man. He'd managed far more responsibility during other hectic seasons. Except in none of those scenarios had he been grieving his brother's passing. Or the loss of a wonderful sister-in-law. He'd never faced the future as a single man solely responsible for the health and well-being of a helpless infant, either. A fist tightened around his heart. What was he going to do? He was so inexperienced, and every day presented new challenges. As soon as he resolved an issue, another one cropped up.

Leaning forward, he took a small sip of coffee, grimacing at the bitter taste. He'd have to invest in something that tasted better than this. Hadn't he passed a coffee shop in town? Trading Post? Add that to his list of questions to ask Rylee.

He opened his email on his laptop. A new message arrived from his friend who was temporarily overseeing the nonprofit dedicated to digging more wells. Evidently, a crew of volunteers from a faith-based organization in North Carolina had just landed in Nicaragua and were ready to get to work.

A wave of excitement washed through him. Sam closed the message. That was great news, but he couldn't get sidetracked tonight. Clean water was his passion. Not planes. He was counting the days until this acquisition was behind him and he could step away from Frazier Aviation. Except, what about Rylee? What would happen to her job? Once Hearts Bay Aviation was acquired and folded into the Frazier brand, Sam couldn't be certain there wouldn't be staffing changes. Sam closed his eyes. He didn't want to think about it. What if after all this, he did his best work, but it had a negative impact on her livelihood? He'd never forgive himself.

Chapter Five

This was exactly what she'd vowed she wouldn't do. Spend too much time with Sam. Except, now they were having lunch together two days in a row. Crystal's birthday wasn't an event she wanted to miss, though. Besides, until Paul and Libby flew in this afternoon, someone had to show the guy around the island.

Rylee worked her way along the table where Crystal's family had put out a spread, loading her paper plate. A baby's cry pulled her attention toward the nearby picnic table where Sam stood with Silas wedged on his hip, a backpack slung over his shoulder, and a small portable high chair in his free hand.

A frown marred his handsome features as he struggled to comfort Silas and manage the gear he'd carried from his SUV. Wow, he was a kind friend bringing a fussy infant to a picnic lunch. Maybe what he needed today was the solidarity of a community of people who could help him out.

She plucked a diet soda from the cooler on the ground beside the table, then made her way toward Sam and Silas.

"Hey." Rylee set down her plate filled with a cheeseburger, potato salad and fresh berries.

"Hi." Sam had placed Silas in the chair. He didn't look up as he fumbled with the straps and buckles. Silas fussed louder and kicked his legs.

Rylee hesitated. She didn't feel right tucking into her meal when Sam looked like he might need a hand. "Is there anything I can do to help?"

Sam shook his head. "Believe it or not, I've got this under control."

"All right." Rylee plucked the plasticware and napkin she'd tucked in her back pocket and settled on the worn wooden bench.

Sam slid a plastic tray onto the chair, then secured a bib around Silas's neck. The baby glanced at Rylee and offered her an unexpected smile.

"Well, aren't you the cutest thing?" She walked her fingers slowly across the table and gently tugged on the toe of his gray sock. Silas squealed. She pulled her hand away, then walked her fingers across the table and jiggled his foot. He squealed louder and started to giggle.

Rylee chuckled. She couldn't resist repeating the process. Silas's belly laugh drew some curious glances and friendly smiles from the handful of people sitting at nearby tables.

Sam shot her a mock glare. "Are you about done distracting the boy from his meal?"

"I'm sorry. What was the question?" Rylee grinned. "That belly laugh is captivating."

"Maybe you could pick this game back up later? It takes me almost forty-five minutes to feed him, so I need to get started."

Rylee grimaced. "I really am sorry. Do you want me to get you a plate of food? Or something to drink?"

Sam shook his head. "I'll grab something in a bit."

She popped the top on her diet soda.

Sam retrieved the small container of baby food from his backpack. When Silas spotted it, his adorable nose scrunched and he started to cry.

"I know. I'm working on it, buddy." Sam held up a spoon. "Give me a minute, okay?"

The sound of Crystal's laughter filtered through the cool air. "They seem so happy together, don't they?"

Sam hesitated, a spoonful of something orange and soupy halfway to Silas's mouth. "To be honest, I haven't seen Josh and Crystal together very much."

"Have you met Crystal?"

"Once," Sam said. "We had lunch in Seattle last year when she and Josh were in town visiting some friends."

Rylee unfolded her napkin and spread it on her lap, then picked up her cheeseburger.

Sam carefully spooned tiny portions of pureed fruit into Silas's mouth. Part of it came right back out on the bib. Sam sighed and tried again.

Rylee had spent quite a bit of time with her sisters' children, but somehow she had managed to avoid ever having to feed them anything more than a bottle. "Adding solids is quite the process, isn't it?"

Sam nodded. "He slept so much better last night, though. I can't believe the difference. Mia was so right about starting solids and changing the formula."

"I'll let her know. She'll be happy to hear that Silas is doing better."

She took a bite of her burger, savoring the delicious combination of a grilled patty, melted cheese, along with crisp lettuce and a juicy tomato slice squeezed between a brioche bun. Bits and pieces of Chelsea and Crystal's conversation swirled around her. At the next table, they discussed honeymoon plans, Crystal's hopes of still finding the perfect going away outfit before they left for Mexico, and how many swimsuits she planned to pack. Chelsea hung on every word and offered plenty of suggestions.

Rylee had to stifle the urge to roll her eyes. Exhibit A of why she hadn't wanted to be the maid of honor. It wasn't that she didn't care about Crystal and Josh's plans. She just wasn't real interested in hashing out all the details. She shifted her attention back to Sam and Silas. After loading her fork with potato salad, she tried not to overanalyze why she'd rather talk to this guy she hardly knew while he fed a baby instead of hang with her closest friend.

Jealousy?

She shook off the notion. It didn't usually bother her to be one of the unmarried girls in her local friend group. Work kept her busy, especially in the summer, and she enjoyed the adventure of flying. And sometimes it was nice not to have to think about a relationship. But for some reason as they got closer and closer to Josh and Crystal's wedding, she found herself focusing more on the fact that she was single. Sure, it was by choice, but also because she was still protecting her wounded heart. She'd never been overly cautious about anything.

Until the Tucker debacle.

Maybe Sam and Silas sitting next to her had shifted her focus to romance and commitment. Not that she was truly ready for that. Especially not with a guy who had unexpectedly become a baby's guardian. Besides, Sam had more than enough to deal with right now. He didn't strike her as even remotely interested in dating. And especially not someone who worked at Hearts Bay Aviation.

Sam patiently offered Silas another bite of fruit. "Are you going fishing after lunch?"

"No," Rylee said, smothering a laugh as Silas blew raspberries and sprayed Sam's hand with baby food. "I'm working this afternoon."

"Silas, no." Sam shook his head and wiped his hand with a napkin. "Where are you headed today?"

"I'm delivering mail and groceries to a fishing lodge on a remote part of the island. Are you going fishing?"

"Absolutely not. Now that I know this kid can nap…well, I'm going to give him every opportunity to sleep as long as he wants to. Besides, I have my first meeting with Paul and Libby at four o'clock."

"Have you found someone to babysit yet?"

She took a sip of her soda. From the corner of her eye, she spotted Chelsea approaching.

"Rylee, we're going to get manicures and pedicures this afternoon. Would you like to join us? Everyone else is going fishing."

Rylee swallowed, letting the carbonated liquid coat her throat, then put the can back on the picnic table. "I wish I could but I have to work."

"Oh." Chelsea frowned. "I assumed you had the day off."

"Nope. Sorry. I'll take…"

Never mind. She didn't bother finishing her explanation. Chelsea didn't need to know her vacation plans.

The girl wasn't paying attention anyway. Chelsea's gaze had already shifted to Sam. Her smile widened. "This must be the best man I've heard so much about."

Sam's kind eyes pinged from her outstretched hand to the baby food and spoon he held, then back to Chelsea. "Sam Frazier. And you are?"

"I'm Chelsea, Crystal's cousin." She let her hand rest on Sam's shoulder as she leaned in and spoke nonsense to Silas. "And your son is the most adorable thing I've ever seen. Hi, handsome! Are you a good eater? Yes, you are."

Rylee had to tighten her grip around her drink to keep from removing Chelsea's hand from Sam's shoulder. That was petty, but she couldn't handle the ridiculous flirting. Or the juvenile baby talk.

"I didn't realize you were a single dad, Sam," Chelsea said, reaching in to tap her finger on Silas's nose.

Silas's face crumpled and he burst into tears.

"Hey, Chelsea. Josh is calling you. They need another person to play cornhole." Rylee tipped her head toward the impromptu game starting nearby.

Chelsea giggled and nudged Rylee's shoulder with her hip. "No, he's not. Silly. Josh knows I don't like cornhole."

Rylee stifled a groan.

"It was nice meeting you." Sam stood and reached for a napkin. "Excuse me while I help this little guy finish his lunch."

"Of course." Chelsea beamed and tossed her hair. "I can't wait to hear more about you and that sweet baby boy."

Hoping she'd take the hint, Rylee waggled her fingers at Chelsea, which elicited a glare before Chelsea flounced away.

Sam's amused gaze held hers. "I'm guessing the two of you are close?"

"Great guess. You're right." Rylee took a generous bite of her potato salad to keep from saying something regrettable. Why did she even care if Chelsea flirted with Sam? Rylee wasn't interested in him. She refused to date a man who'd soon be her employer. Sam seemed like a nice guy, and Chelsea liked to flirt even though she wasn't ready for a serious commitment, especially with a single father. That's why this annoyed her, Rylee thought, because she didn't want to see a good guy get hurt. Not because she was interested in Sam. Not at all.

"Come on, you've got time for one game." Josh grinned and pressed a beanbag into Sam's hand.

Sam hesitated, glancing over his shoulder. Rylee stood near the picnic table with Silas nestled on her shoulder. Eating lunch must've taken a lot out of him because he'd fallen asleep in her arms a few minutes ago. She flashed him a smile and a thumbs-up. His heart thrummed.

Wow, she looked good holding Silas.

He banished the thought, smiled, and held up the beanbag. Josh had coerced him into playing, and Sam couldn't deny that he'd been having a good time. But Rylee had to go back to work soon, and Sam wasn't about to shirk his responsibilities. She'd already gone out of her way to rescue him plenty of times.

She lifted one shoulder, then nodded approval.

"Hello." Josh waved his hand in front of Sam's face. "Do you want to play or not?"

"I'm in." Sam lined up beside Josh. Crystal and her mom stood beside the opposite cornhole frame, chatting. He should really get ready for his meeting with Paul and Libby. For a guy who'd come here to acquire a company, he sure hadn't invested much time analyzing the purchase.

"You and Rylee seem to be getting along well," Josh said, taking a sip of his soda.

"Rylee and her family have been extremely gracious," Sam said. "Silas had a health issue that I didn't know about, and I was at my wit's end with a baby who wouldn't stop crying. Worse, he kept getting sick. So Rylee's sister Mia treated him and now he's like a completely different kid."

"That's awesome." Josh turned and tossed the blue beanbag across the lawn. It sailed through the hole in the frame. "That's one great thing about this place. People pull together and help out."

"Yeah? What else is great about this island?"

Josh chucked the next beanbag toward the cornhole board. "When the sun shines, this town is beautiful. Friendly people, fairly low crime rate and plenty of great outdoor activities."

Sam stepped forward. It was his turn. The beanbag sailed through the air and landed softly in the grass beside the board. Oh, brother.

"What don't you like?"

Josh shot him a curious glance. "Why do you ask?"

Sam shrugged. "Just making conversation. You're marrying a girl who grew up here. Any plans to settle down in Hearts Bay?"

Josh chuckled. "Did Crystal's mom tell you to ask me that?"

"Nope."

"Crystal likes teaching school in Anchorage. My job as an occupational therapist is very rewarding and I have more than enough patients, so I don't feel the need to relocate." Josh's gaze slid toward Rylee. "Are you interested in settling down in Hearts Bay?"

Sam hesitated before tossing his second beanbag. It landed on the edge of the frame and then slid off onto the grass. Crystal and her mother high-fived.

"I don't have any plans to leave Seattle," Sam said.

"But Frazier Aviation is probably going to acquire Rylee's company, right? So I imagine your family will have to relocate staff here."

"I'm not part of that equation," Sam said, frowning as Crystal's gray beanbag sailed through the hole in the frame near his feet.

"So your role here is to tie up any loose ends,

finalize the acquisition, then go back to Seattle?" Josh asked.

"Right." Sam nodded and resisted the urge to glance at Rylee again. A small part of him was relieved she wasn't standing close enough to hear what he'd said. Not that he wasn't being honest. He didn't plan to stay on Orca Island, and his father hadn't invited him to share his thoughts on who should step into the role of general manager. Frankly, Sam didn't have an opinion on that. Once he left, that problem wasn't his to consider. But it was better for everyone involved if current employees didn't hear this conversation. Especially Rylee.

Crystal and her mother nailed three of their four tosses. Josh and Sam had some work to do if they wanted to win.

Focus.

He already had a team waiting for him to devote all his attention to the villagers' needs in Nicaragua. There was no way he'd undo all those plans. For all the reasons Josh mentioned about staying in Anchorage after he and Crystal got married, Sam could say the same was true for him and his home base. Besides, he'd need all the support he could get back in Seattle to help Silas grow and thrive.

Except you've already received plenty of support here.

His stomach knotted. Folks had been quick to rescue him. Without criticizing or judging his ineptitude about Silas's care. Kindness like that was hard to come by. He bungled his next two beanbag tosses. Crystal and her mom ended up winning. Sam excused himself from playing another round. Clearly, his heart wasn't in it. His thoughts and emotions were so conflicted about his future. Especially when he locked eyes with Rylee still holding Silas. Sunshine peeked through mottled clouds. The aroma of grilled burgers and hotdogs still lingered in the air. He detoured to the food table and grabbed two chocolate-chip cookies.

He'd never been a picnic-lunch-in-the-middle-of-the-workday kind of guy. But ever since he'd lost his brother and sister-in-law and become a single parent overnight, he'd been pausing to reflect more often. Maybe that's what grief did to a person. Made them evaluate everything through the lens of loss. Now when he made decisions, he had to think of what was best for Silas.

And, selfishly, what was best for himself. What he truly wanted.

Because what he wanted was a partner. Not for pedestrian reasons, like an extra set of hands to care for Silas, but for meaningful connection too. It had never bothered him that he was a bachelor until this summer. Until he had held his distraught nephew, panic welling inside because he couldn't soothe the little guy's heartache.

Rylee hadn't moved from her spot beside the picnic table. A woman Sam didn't know had approached, and Rylee swayed back and forth, keeping her voice low while she spoke. Silas slept in her arms. He had his cheek pressed against Rylee's shoulder and his mouth hung open.

So adorable.

Sam sat at the picnic table and put one cookie on the napkin for Rylee. He took a bite of the other and tried to enjoy the chewy treat without eavesdropping. No matter how much he worried about meeting Silas's needs, he was confident that this was not the right time to start dating someone new. He polished off the cookie. Rylee was a wonderful woman and a natural with children. But their time together was fleeting and a relationship between them wasn't meant to be.

Later that day, Rylee stood in the hangar at the edge of the airport property, reviewing her emergency preparedness checklist. After lunch at the park, then her mail and medication run to the west side of the island, she'd landed at the airport just in time to greet Paul and Libby. They were right on schedule to meet with Sam. It wasn't any of her business what her bosses discussed with Sam Frazier, but she was curious, so she was taking her time checking her first-aid kit and restocking. Still, it would be super obvious if she hung around for too long. Paul and Libby knew that this task didn't take more than thirty minutes. Although, thoughts of sitting with Sam during lunch at the park threatened to steal her concentration, forcing her to keep rechecking the same items over and over again.

Vacuum splints? Check. Ax? Check. Flares, an Automated External Defibrillator and a Mylar blanket. All packed and in working order. Next, she examined the tarp, made sure she had at least two bottles of insect-repellent spray and two liters of water. She stowed the first-aid kit and the rest of the supplies in the back of the Cessna airplane, then climbed out and leaped to the concrete floor.

Carson needed the aircraft first thing in the morning, so she planned to speak with him before she went home. Maybe she'd grab a pizza from Maverick's, head to her place and watch a few episodes of *Virgin River*.

Anything to keep Sam and Silas from taking up residence in her thoughts.

Humming a popular country song she'd heard on the radio this morning, Rylee crossed the asphalt toward the employee entrance of the airport. Libby stood in the doorway, wearing a white and navy blue floral blouse and navy blue slacks. She had her strawberry blonde hair pinned up in its trademark bun, a pencil stuck inside the thick coil of hair, and gold hoop earrings dangled from her lobes.

"Hey, Libby, you look nice today. All set for your meeting with Sam Frazier?"

"Thank you, dear." Libby patted her on the arm. "As ready as we'll ever be. Still can't believe we're going through with this."

"That makes two of us," Rylee said softly. Unexpected tears surfaced and she blinked them back.

Libby's chin wobbled but she held it together. "Thanks so much for keeping an eye on things while Paul and I were away. It gave us a sense of peace knowing you and Carson were here."

Rylee cleared the lump in her throat. "No problem. Everything went smoothly."

"We knew it would."

Rylee followed Libby inside the airport. Were she and Paul having doubts about the sale? Seemed a bit late for that. From what she'd been told, this was basically a done deal. Sam had come to Hearts Bay to fulfill the due diligence obligations.

Whatever that meant.

"Say, do you happen to have any contact information for Sam Frazier?"

Uh-oh. "I do. Is everything okay?"

"Hope so," Libby said, circling behind their customer service desk. "He hasn't showed up for the meeting yet, and he's twenty minutes late."

"Let me see what's going on." She stood on the opposite side of the desk and pulled her phone from her pocket. "Rats, I missed a call from him."

Before she could listen to the voice mail, the automatic doors behind her parted and Sam strode in with a fussy Silas in his arms and a backpack slung over his shoulder.

"I'm so sorry," Sam said. "My babysitter got sick and she couldn't recommend a sub. I didn't know who else to call."

Libby offered a polite smile. "Oh, my. What a day you're having."

He let the backpack drop to the floor and held out his hand. "Hi, you must be Libby. I'm Sam Frazier."

"It's nice to meet you, Sam." Libby shook his hand. "Welcome to Hearts Bay."

"Thank you, and again, I am so incredibly sorry. I don't want to reschedule, but I would understand if you wanted to. Babies don't really belong in business meetings."

"I can help." Rylee held out her arms. "Come here, sweet boy."

Silas grinned and leaned toward her.

"Wait. Are you sure?" Sam frowned and awkwardly shifted Silas in his arms. "I can't ask you to do that."

"You didn't ask. I offered." She took Silas and settled him on her hip, breathing in the scent of baby shampoo or wipes or whatever that delightful fragrance was that she couldn't seem to get enough of. "Give me your bag. I'll take care of him."

"Where?"

"Oh, don't you worry. I know people on the island who have baby-friendly houses. We'll start with my sister Lexi. You don't mind if Silas is near a dog, do you?"

"No, not at all." Sam palmed the back of his neck. "What about his car seat?"

"Yikes, I hadn't thought about that."

Sam's features pinched. "I didn't put any other drivers on my rental contract, so I can't lend you the car. Do you know how to trade out an infant car seat base?"

"I do." Libby tipped her head toward the door. "Why don't I help Rylee move the car seat to her car? And you go on in to the office there and start chatting with Paul."

"See? That all worked out." Rylee grinned. "Text me when you're finished. I'll give you my sister's address."

"Thank you." Sam pulled his keys from his coat pocket and handed them over. "Seriously, you have no idea how much this means to me."

"It's no trouble." Rylee walked her fingers up Silas's tummy and gently tickled him under his chin. "Come on, little buddy. Let's go have some fun."

His infectious baby laugh echoed off the walls of the airport, drawing amused glances from passengers moving toward the ticket counter nearby.

"Lexi and Molly Jo will have all kinds of toys for you to play with."

Silas tucked two fingers in his mouth.

"That's right. We're going to go for a short ride."

Sidestepping a family of four towing their suitcases through the airport's front doors, Rylee and Libby walked outside. A late-afternoon breeze had kicked up and the air was cool.

"I hope Silas is warm enough in these pajamas." Rylee paused and peeked inside the backpack. "Maybe there's a blanket or a jacket inside this thing."

"He seems like a nice guy," Libby said. "I didn't realize he was a single dad."

"Long story short, Silas is his nephew." She pressed the button on the key fob. The SUV chirped and its lights blinked. "Yep. This is the one. Let's get your car seat, pumpkin."

Libby peered through the window. "Oh, yeah. We can handle this."

"I'm glad you know what to do. I can sort of take care of a baby, but I have no idea how to install a car seat."

"It's a bit of a hassle, but I can get it," Libby said.

True to her word, less than fifteen minutes later, she had the contraption safely installed in Rylee's car.

Libby stood beside the open back door and tucked a strand of hair behind her ear. "Infants have to ride facing backward. You probably knew that already. Do you know how to put him in there?"

Rylee hesitated. "Maybe you should show me how."

"Come on, cutie patootie." Libby scooped Silas into her arms. He started to cry.

"Aww, poor thing. Don't worry," Rylee said, hovering outside the vehicle. "I'm right here. We're going to have so much fun together."

Libby got him settled, buckled his harness,

and gave him the pacifier attached to a stuffed monkey.

"Where did you find that?" Rylee asked.

Libby closed the door. "It was in the car seat."

"Thank you so much." Rylee handed over Sam's keys. "Hope you have a great meeting with Sam."

"Hope you have a good time with that cute little baby." Libby squeezed her arm, took the car keys and returned to the airport.

Rylee tucked the backpack into her trunk, then slipped behind the wheel of her car, suddenly anxious. She'd driven her nieces and nephews around before, but somehow this felt different. They'd always been bigger. More self-sufficient. Precious Silas needed to be cared for and protected.

"It's all right. You can do hard things, remember?"

She fished her phone from her coat pocket and texted her sister Lexi.

Hey, I know this is completely last minute. Can I come over and bring a baby?

Lexi's response arrived quickly.

Of course. I can't wait to hear how you were put in charge of a baby. Heath's out of town, so I'm going to order pizza. You're welcome to stay.

She punched the air with her fist. Lexi to the rescue. What would she do without her family to rely on? Thankfully, as long as she lived here, she'd never have to find out.

But what if you can't stay?

Gritting her teeth against the doubt that swirled in like a January blizzard, obliterating all rational thought, she put her phone down and started the car. Sure, Sam had asked a few questions about staffing, but that didn't mean he valued what she and Carson and their co-workers did every day. For all she knew, once he resigned, the leadership in Seattle might cut back from five and a half pilots to three or fewer, just to save money. It wouldn't be the first time outside organizations showed up and unraveled all the well-ordered plans that locals had put in place.

She white-knuckled the steering wheel the entire drive to Lexi and Heath's house. Rarely did she encounter sexist attitudes at work. The men who flew with her and worked for her competitors off-island had always been friendly and respectful. But she wasn't naïve. She'd fought hard to carve out her role in the small company, and there was no way she'd leave without advocating for herself. If someone's position had to be eliminated, though, Carson had worked there longer. The other pilots all had more experience than she did. Doubt gnawed at her insides. She'd just have to take advantage of every opportunity to show Sam that she was a skilled pilot, then pray that he gave the leadership back in Seattle a favorable report.

How embarrassing.

Sam followed the instructions on the GPS toward the home where Rylee had said she and Silas were waiting. He blew out a long breath, rubbing his fingertips against the throbbing ache in his forehead. His family should have sent someone else to manage this acquisition. There was probably a summer intern at Frazier's headquarters who could've done a better job convincing Paul and Libby to accept the offer.

He wouldn't be at all surprised if they declined. He had been a flustered distracted mess, and he knew the sale of this company was not just about getting a good financial return for the Suttons. They wanted to make sure they were selling to a business that would keep their well-run organization serving its customers well. He'd hardly exuded professionalism with his late arrival, baby in tow and thoughts scattered. Finally toward the middle of the conversation, he'd found his stride. After Libby had joined them, handed over his keys, then reassured him that Silas and Rylee would be fine, he'd relaxed. Delivered what his father and the board of directors back in Seattle had asked him to do.

But he didn't feel great about it.

If Paul and Libby declined this offer, they'd have to find another buyer. That only made him feel one hundred times worse, because they seemed like an amazing couple. They cared about the community and wanted to make sure that Hearts Bay would still receive a comparable level of service if Frazier Aviation took over. Sam had never given much thought to aviation's essential role in helping Alaskans survive and thrive. Now that he'd spent some time on Orca Island, he'd realized that the rugged terrain and challenging weather conditions tested pilots' skills, yet they still managed to get the job done.

The GPS indicated he'd almost arrived at his destination. He slowed down and pulled into a driveway in front of a lovely one-level rambler. The lush green lawn had been recently mowed. Blooming flowers spilled from two hanging baskets near the front door. Sam parked beside Rylee's car, turned off the ignition and exited the vehicle.

Through the wide front window, he spotted Rylee and another woman inside sitting on the floor. He slowed his steps. They hadn't noticed him yet. Rylee smiled, then tipped her head back, obviously laughing. Warmth spread through his chest. Wow, she was so pretty.

The woman glanced up and met his gaze with her own. Rats. Caught. He managed a sheepish wave. She waved back and pushed to her feet.

Somewhere close by, a dog barked. Then the door opened and a young woman who resembled Rylee greeted him. "Hi. I'm Lexi Donovan, Rylee's sister."

"Sam Frazier." He shook her outstretched hand. "It's nice to meet you, Lexi. Thanks for hosting the playdate."

"Anytime. Please come in." She had her hair piled on top of her head and wore a red T-shirt and denim shorts. Her oversized hoop earrings bobbed as she stepped back and motioned for him to join them.

Sam stepped inside and took off his shoes.

"May I take your jacket?" Lexi asked.

"Thank you." He shrugged off his coat and handed it to Lexi. She tucked it away in a closet nearby.

"Silas is adorable, by the way." Lexi closed the closet door. "He and Molly Jo are having a great time together."

Rylee glanced up and smiled. "Hey."

"Hey." Sam padded over. "I'm sorry, the meeting ran long."

Her smile dimmed and something he couldn't quite name flickered in her eyes. "No problem. Silas has found his new favorite toy."

On the floor beside Rylee, Silas sat on a blanket. He had a blue plastic block shoved in his mouth. A brown-haired toddler with blue eyes peeked up at him, then went back to wrapping her doll in a tiny pink blanket.

He turned toward Lexi. "How old's your daughter?"

Lexi sat cross-legged on the floor. "She'll be two in December, and I've got one on the way."

"Congratulations," Sam said.

"Thank you." Lexi handed Molly Jo a small bottle. "Would you like to feed your baby before you leave?"

Molly Jo nodded, then took the bottle and sank into Lexi's lap, clutching the swaddled doll in her arms.

"Molly Jo is going to stay with our sister Tess tonight. Our niece Lucy wanted to try having a sleepover," Rylee said. She and Lexi exchanged smiles. "How do you think that will go?"

Lexi grimaced. "I'm afraid she will want to come home in the middle of the night, which will be a bummer because Heath's out of town and, selfishly, I don't want to have to go get her. This pregnant mama needs her sleep."

Rylee smoothed her hand over Silas's head. "If you need help, give me a call. I can pick her up and bring her home."

"Aww, that's sweet of you. Thank you." Lexi glanced up at Sam. "Would you like to sit down?"

"Uh, sure." He did feel silly, standing there, hovering. Is this how playdates worked? Slowly, he sank onto one end of the sofa nearby.

"Ba, ba, ba." Silas held the slobbery block out to Rylee.

"That's a block, you're right." Rylee bopped his nose with the tip of her finger.

He giggled and then shoved the corner of the block back into his mouth.

"He's been doing great." Rylee's gaze found Sam's again. "Lexi helped me figure out how to feed him. I hope that's okay with you."

Sam checked the time on his smartwatch. "Oh, wow. Yeah, I'm sure he was hungry. It's six thirty already."

"We saved some pizza for you," Lexi said.

Sam held up his hands. "No, thank you, I don't want to intrude."

"You're not." Rylee pinned him with a long look. "There's plenty of pizza, plus salad, and Lexi made pie for dessert."

"Are you sure it's no trouble?" Sam's stomach growled.

Lexi chuckled. "No trouble at all. Like I said, my husband's out of town, so you'll be doing me a favor by eating some of what's left over. Besides, I hear your tummy growling."

He pinched the back of his neck with his hand. "It's been a while since lunch."

"You can eat and enjoy your meal. We'll keep Silas occupied." Lexi stood and moved toward the kitchen. "Give me a few minutes and I'll have a plate fixed for you."

"Thank you again." Sam slumped back on the sofa. "Clearly, I need all the help I can get."

Rylee's brows slanted. "What do you mean?"

"I showed up at an important meeting with a baby, and now I'm mooching dinner from another one of your family members."

She lifted one shoulder in a casual shrug. "Lots of people have to juggle meetings and childcare issues. Your babysitter was very considerate to let you know she had a fever."

"True."

"Paul and Libby have kids and grandkids. They understand. The whole reason for selling their business is because their family needs help."

"Thank you for being so gracious," Sam said. His parents would be mortified if they knew how poorly he was handling all of this. Nothing about his behavior reflected well on Frazier Aviation. Dad had never specifically stated Sam shouldn't leave the company. His disappointment had been evident, though. Now that Lucas was gone, Sam carried the burden of making sure this deal went through. Except today had not gone at all like he'd hoped.

He'd do better. He had to. Because there was no way he'd go back to Seattle a failure.

Chapter Six

If she had to tie a bow on one more miniature bottle of bubbles, she just might scream.

Rylee sat at the table in the community center with six boxes of the bubble bottles spread out on the table. Crystal sat across from her along with five other women from Hearts Bay Community Church who'd volunteered to help.

They had two weeks before the wedding reception. But tying small pieces of ribbon in little bows had never been her gift. At the rate she was going, they'd finish just in time to attend the rehearsal.

"If I ever get married, remind me to elope. No bubbles needed for the reception, no stress about how much food the caterer needs and no—"

"No memories for your family and friends who want to be a part of your big day," Crystal interrupted, giving her the stink eye. "You are by far the grumpiest member of the bridal party."

Oof. That hurt. "I'm sorry. You're right. I need to work on my attitude." Rylee managed to get the end of the ribbon threaded through the small hole on the oval sign that read "Mr. and Mrs."

"At least this gives us time to catch up," Crystal said. "How have you been? It seems like you're busy what with Paul and Libby selling the company. How do you feel about that?"

Rylee reached for her coffee. Crystal had stopped by The Trading Post and picked up drinks and scones. A little encouragement to help her stay motivated. Her best friend knew her well. Sweets and caffeine always did the trick. She took a long sip, then set her drink down.

"Works been good. Mostly."

"Yeah?" Crystal's eyes sparkled with amusement. "Sam's been the talk of the town."

"Really? I hadn't noticed."

"Ha." Crystal unboxed a dozen more bottles of bubbles and slid six across the table toward Rylee.

"Can't we just throw birdseed or rice?" Rylee asked.

"No, it's not good for the environment. Besides, I want bubbles. My first choice was sparklers, but my dad said no."

"Oh, sparklers would be fun." Rylee rubbed her palms together. "And no bows or signs to attach."

"When you get married, you can have sparklers," Crystal teased. "Now you have something to look forward to."

Rylee quirked her lips to one side. "That's the thing. I don't know that I'll ever get married."

Conversation screeched to a halt. All heads turned her way. Wow, that certainly sparked a reaction.

Crystal frowned. "Don't you want a husband and a family?"

Rylee paused and let her gaze slide around the table. No one even tried to hide their curiosity. "I don't know for sure."

"So would now be a bad time to point out that you and Sam are getting along well?"

Rylee secured another bow with a tag around the neck of the bottle. Score one for the grouchy MOH. "Sam's nice. If I have to hang out with someone who's going to buy Paul and Libby's business, I'm glad it's a kind, respectful guy."

"Oh, so you do like him?"

Rylee groaned and reached for her coffee. "Your matchmaking schemes are not going to work with me, Crystal."

The rest of the women around the table gradually went back to their own conversations, but Crystal clearly wasn't backing down. She leaned closer. "He's polite and respectful. Josh says that Sam's family is extremely successful and Sam has tons of friends."

"But did you know he doesn't really seem to care that much about airplanes?"

"Josh mentioned that." Crystal punctured the air with her well-manicured finger. "But that's because he's into humanitarian work. Is there anything more admirable?"

"You tell me. You're the one marrying an occupational therapist."

Crystal fixed her with an exasperated look. "Don't try to distract me. Sam is a stand-up guy. Tell me one thing that you've found wrong with him."

Oy. So awkward. Rylee squirmed in her chair. "I don't see anything wrong with him."

"So there's a chance then?"

"A chance of what?"

"That you'll go out. That there's a spark." Crystal set the spool of ribbon aside and picked up her coffee. "I want you to find your happily-ever-after, Rylee."

"If you think introducing me to Sam Frazier is the start of our happily-ever-after, I'd like to remind you that he's not interested in island life."

"When did he say that?"

"He doesn't have to. You can tell. He's only here for three reasons."

Crystal eyed her doubtfully over the plastic lid on her coffee cup.

"Don't look at me like that. He has a packed itinerary." Rylee splayed her hand out, ticking off Sam's objectives one by one. "He's here to serve as Josh's best man, supervise the acquisition, and keep a tiny human alive. He'll be leaving on the eighteenth, so I'm not getting invested in this."

"All right, all right. You've made your point."

Have I, though?

Rylee picked up another handful of Mr. and Mrs. signs, but what little enthusiasm she'd dredged up to finish the project had evaporated when Crystal had brought up Sam.

Crystal set her coffee down. "One more thing and then I'll back off."

"Promise?"

"I want to hear you say that you're willing to consider dating someone again."

"Sure. No problem. I'm willing to consider dating someone," Rylee said with almost zero emotion.

Irritation shadowed Crystal's smile. "So enthusiastic."

"It's going to have to be the right person, Crystal. We've been over this a dozen times. As for Sam—he and I are too different. Our plans, our outlook on life, our—"

"Really? That's all you've got?" Crystal's palm slapped the table.

Rylee flinched.

"Stop making excuses. He loves the Lord. I know you do too. You both adore your families and value hard work. His family owns an aviation company. So help me understand why all of that is a deal-breaker for you."

"Pardon me for interrupting." An older woman's voice echoed through the room.

"Oh, no." Crystal's eyes shuttered and her spine went rigid.

Rylee turned to see Mrs. Lovell, the island's resident curmudgeon, filling the doorway. "You girls are going to have to pack this up and move along. The quilting club is meeting in here in ten minutes."

"No, I have this room reserved for another hour, Mrs. Lovell." Crystal shoved back her chair and stood. "Check the calendar at the front desk."

"Well, plans change, don't they? I had to move the quilting club meeting because there's book club tonight and folks don't appreciate being overscheduled."

"That's not my problem," Crystal said. "I reserved the room and paid the rental fee."

Mrs. Lovell's expression shriveled with bitterness. "That's the problem with you young people. You're so sassy and opinionated these days."

Rylee fended off a laugh.

"And you, young lady." Mrs. Lovell wiggled her bony finger at Rylee. "You need to watch out. That young man with a baby is up to no good."

A chill raced down Rylee's spine. Nothing good ever came from Mrs. Lovell's meddling.

"I don't appreciate these bigwigs from Seattle swooping in and shaking things up." Mrs. Lovell clutched the lapels of her cardigan sweater and pulled them around her.

"It's an acquisition, Mrs. Lovell." Rylee scooped up the remaining crumbs from her scone and deposited them in a napkin. "The company is required to send a representative to oversee the process."

Crystal shot her a "don't bother explaining the details" look.

Rylee shrugged and stood. She didn't like it when the grumpy woman showed up uninvited and tried to control things, but in this case, she secretly appreciated the interruption. The abrupt end of her conversation with Crystal gave her space to escape any further talk of Sam.

"I'll see you later, Crystal." Rylee boxed up the tagged bubbles, then deposited her trash in the can by the door.

Mrs. Lovell blocked her path. "You mark my words. This won't end well. Tell Paul and Libby they'd better give this more careful thought."

Rylee tipped her chin up and challenged Mrs. Lovell's eagle-eyed expression. "Feel free to tell Paul and Libby whatever you'd like. I'm sure they'd be thrilled to hear your thoughts."

Without waiting for an answer, Rylee slipped past Mrs. Lovell and strode down the hall toward the exit. Ninety-nine percent of the time, living in Hearts Bay brought her incredible joy and satisfaction. But every now and then, Mrs. Lovell or some other overbearing resident stirred the pot and created drama.

And as much as she wanted to dismiss everything she'd just heard, Crystal's and Mrs. Lovell's comments left her feeling unsettled. Probably because part of what both women had said felt sort of true. Not that Sam was here under false pretenses or to provoke trouble. But Mrs. Lovell had been partially correct. This merger would shake things up. Sam might be a kind, morally upstanding man, but that didn't mean he would advocate for her to keep her job. Outside, summer sunshine warmed her skin as she strode across the parking lot to her vehicle. Crystal's not-so-subtle nudge that she should consider a relationship with Sam wasn't easy to ignore, either. Because what if Crystal was right?

Sam sat on a bench in the resort's courtyard, one foot braced on the bottom of Silas's stroller, gliding it back and forth.

His technique wasn't helping.

Silas had been crying for at least twenty minutes, and it felt like twenty hours. The scent of pine trees hung in the air. Sunlight bathed the tables, chairs and asphalt walking path in its yellow glow. Perfect weather to be outside, but Silas was not at all impressed.

Sam kept rocking the stroller gently side to side with his foot, and tried to catch up on his email. He half expected a well-meaning guest or staff member to wander over and ask him to make the crying stop. If only it were that easy. He'd tried everything. And if he stayed in that suite another minute with a cranky kid? Well, he wasn't sure how he'd cope.

He'd been tempted but he wasn't about to call on any of the Maddens to rescue him. Not this time. Somehow, he had to get a handle on this single parent thing. Didn't most dads struggle with caring for a cranky infant? Mia had gently suggested that introducing solid food and changing formula would require some time. That he couldn't expect a noticeable difference immediately. And yet that's exactly what he'd hoped for. For a while, it had seemed to work too. Silas was sleeping better, and most of the time he was happy and quiet. It was those other times that still bothered him.

If he'd learned one thing already, it was that caring for a baby was going to teach him valuable lessons about adjusting his expectations.

His phone chimed and he glanced at his inbox.

Thankfully, Silas had settled a bit. Sam leaned forward and peeked inside the stroller. As soon as he'd made eye contact with Silas, the crying ramped up.

Rookie mistake.

"How about a pacifier?" He tried giving it to him.

Face flushed, Silas turned away and arched his back.

"Stuffed animal?" Sam held up the small, soft, green frog.

Silas kicked his feet hard, thrusting the blanket aside.

"I guess that's a no." Sam tossed the stuffed animal in the basket under the stroller and tried readjusting the blanket. He angled the sunshade. Nothing satisfied this kid. "How about another walk?"

Why did he even bother *asking*? He stood and pushed the stroller along the paved path, moving slowly so he could read the message in his inbox from one of his closest friends in Seattle, Brandt Douglas. An incredible guy and someone Sam deeply respected. Brandt had checked on him often since his brother and Erin had passed.

Sam quickly scanned the path to make sure no one was coming, then read the message.

Checking in on you, pal. Anything I can do? Hopefully things are going well in Alaska. I know you've got a lot on your plate. I can only imagine how challenging this must be. When you have a few minutes, please give me a call.

Silas had found his fist this time and slurped loudly, his eyelids fluttering.

Sam shook his head in amazement. Maybe all he needed was a change of scenery.

"That makes two of us, kiddo." He scrolled to Brandt's name in his contacts and pressed the button to make the call.

Brandt answered on the second ring. "Sam, my man. How's it going?"

"Hanging in there. You?"

"Can't complain. What's going on in Alaska?"

Sam always admired Brandt's boundless enthusiasm. Exactly what he needed in a moment like this—a wise friend with a solid pep talk. "Things are not great. Struggling with this acquisition, the due diligence period is underway and there are mountains of documents to review."

Brandt released a low whistle. "That's a lot to manage. How is Silas handling the trip?"

Sam risked another glance into the stroller. Silas had fallen asleep. At last.

"He's had better days. We're learning to take life one minute at a time."

"That's the way." Brandt paused. "Listen. There's an article in today's paper that has me a little concerned. I wanted to give you a heads-up."

Sam's stomach tightened. "What kind of an article?"

"It's about your family's business ventures, and it doesn't paint a great picture, my friend. Thought I'd reach out and make sure you were aware."

Sam slowed his steps. Silas's eyes popped open and he started crying. Sam bit back a groan and kept walking. "I appreciate that. Can you send me a link?"

"I will if you want me to."

"Yeah. Let me...let me look it over."

"All right, I'm on it," Brandt said. "If you need anything, give me a call. I'm here for you. You know that, right?"

"Yeah, of course." Sam forced enthusiasm into his voice. "Thanks, man."

"All right. I'll send you that link. Take care, buddy."

"You too." Sam hung up and stared at his phone, willing the link to appear.

As promised, Brandt's message arrived. Sam hesitated, his finger hovering over the link. Then he tapped it and waited for his phone to redirect. The article appeared on his refresh screen. He plowed through the first paragraph. A longtime Seattle journalist, who often wrote analytical opinion pieces on local businesses, didn't mince words. He was skeptical about the future of Frazier Aviation and their ability to function without Sam's brother. There were shortsighted and thoughtless observations about integrity, and the author went so far as to question the company's viability in the highly competitive marketplace. Of course, he hadn't bothered to interview a single member of the family or anyone else on the board of directors. Frankly, the parts Sam had read so far amounted to nothing more than mudslinging.

Sam closed out the browser without finishing the article. Anger burned through his veins. How dare they? Their timing couldn't be worse.

He shoved his phone in his pocket and picked up the pace, wheeling the stroller along the path. But the damage was done. The words had undermined his already fragile confidence. Amid his grief and heartache, he felt like the journalist had kicked him in the teeth.

No matter what people thought or published in the paper, Sam vowed he'd prove them wrong. He wasn't sure how he'd pull that off exactly. Analyze all the documentation from Hearts Bay Aviation that still waited for him on his hard drive? Take that flightseeing tour with Rylee? Interview current employees? The path forward wasn't entirely clear, but somehow he'd do everything necessary to make doubly sure this merger happened. Because there was no way he'd allow a sensational newspaper article packed full of half-truths and misinformation to undermine his family's legacy in Seattle or in the aviation industry.

"Annie, please. You have to help me."

At this point, Rylee wasn't too proud to beg. Or offer to scrub the coffee shop's bathroom floors for the next twenty Saturdays. "I'm way out of my comfort zone here."

Her friend eyed her from across the table they'd claimed inside The Trading Post. "The wedding is only two weeks away, right? How'd you get saddled with planning activities for the guests?"

Rylee blew out a long breath. "Crystal's sister feels bad that she'll be on bed rest and can't come to the wedding, so she and her mom had planned all the details for the shower already. We also spent a weekend in San Diego during Crystal's spring break in March, and she didn't want any additional bachelorette activities. Instead, she asked me to plan something fun for the guests to do together."

Annie drummed her fingertips against the side of her blue ceramic mug. "I'm guessing she expects something more substantial than the usual bridal shower games?"

"One hundred percent. Crystal prefers a half-day itinerary with options for the outdoorsy guests." Rylee used air quotes when mentioning the others. "As well as a more relaxed activity for the older folks or in case it's raining."

Annie frowned. "That's a lot. The bride-to-be might have to adjust her lofty expectations."

"I think it's a bit late in the game to tell her that."

"But Crystal grew up here," Annie insisted. "She knows the weather can be cold and rainy, even in the middle of July. If she wanted a tropical destination experience, she should've—"

"All right, all right." Rylee held up her hand. "If you don't want to brainstorm with me, I'll go ask my sisters."

Annie's expression softened. "I'm sorry. I didn't mean to be so crabby. It just seems like Crystal and Josh are taking advantage of you."

Rylee bit back another protest. Annie knew her too well. Reaching for her plastic cup, she rattled the ice inside and then took a long sip of her frappuccino. The sweet liquid slid down her throat and gave her time to assess Annie's comments. Had Crystal and Josh expected too much? Probably. But she'd already said yes. She didn't want to back out and let them down now.

"I fully acknowledge that I made a questionable choice, but I still need you, Annie. I'm great at wrapping gifts, and I'll try to be a mostly awesome maid of honor, but planning an event that suits guests of all ages and has a backup plan in case of rain feels overwhelming."

A baby's bubbly laugh distracted her. Rylee glanced toward the next table. A young woman held a little one on her lap. The man sitting across from her played an engaging game of peekaboo. Every time he moved his hands away from his face and smiled, the baby girl pointed and laughed. Rylee couldn't help but smile too. Her thoughts immediately shifted to Sam and Silas. What had Sam done about his ongoing childcare issues?

"Hello?" Annie's voice tugged her back to their conversation.

Rylee met her friend's curious gaze. "Sorry. Zoned out there for a second."

"What's on your mind? Or maybe I should ask who is on your mind?"

Warmth heated Rylee's face. "No one. There's a cute baby playing peekaboo. That's all."

"So if I told you that a handsome guy from Seattle with the most adorable baby boy in the world are about to walk in here, you wouldn't care?"

Rylee straightened in her chair and looked around. "They're here? Where?"

"You are interested. I knew it."

Rylee twisted in her seat and surveyed the shop. Sam hadn't come inside yet. She craned her neck to peek through the windows. No sign of him outside, either.

Disappointment planted a hollow ache in her abdomen. She turned back to face Annie. "Not cool. You tricked me."

"I wasn't tricking you." Annie flashed her

a knowing smile. "Just testing a hypothesis. What's going on between you, that handsome stranger and his pint-size sidekick?"

"Nothing," Rylee insisted. "He's here because his family's company is acquiring Hearts Bay Aviation from Paul and Libby. I've been tasked with showing him around and he's needed a helping hand a time or two when a crisis broke out."

"So you're the maid of honor in a wedding when you'd rather be a bridesmaid, your company is being acquired, and this handsome guy with a baby needs your assistance." Annie's expression turned doubtful. "And now you've added special events coordinator to your list of wedding week responsibilities?"

"Which is why I'm asking for your help." Rylee reached across the table and clutched Annie's forearm. "I'll clean your bathroom for a month. Run all your errands. Take your favorite relatives on a trip to Anchorage. *Please* toss me a lifeline here."

"I'll collect when the time is right."

"Deal."

"How about a scavenger hunt but with a twist?"

Rylee hesitated. "What kind of a twist?"

"My parents have a neighbor who lives in Oregon for part of the year. She has a glass-blowing studio. Anyway, my mom says the neighbor has all kinds of glass ornaments that she's made. Evidently, they resemble the glass floats that used to be on fishing boats. What if you organized a scavenger hunt for guests to find the floats that you'd hidden around town?"

Rylee dragged her finger through the condensation collecting on the side of her cup. "That sounds expensive. I don't know if Josh and Crystal want to pay for glass artwork."

"So Josh and Crystal want you to organize a free activity for their guests?"

"Not free. Just not…"

"Fancy? Or is my suggestion too corny?" Annie's brows scrunched together. "You're not giving me much to work with. You said a half-day activity, that people of all ages might enjoy and could also be done in rainy weather. So why doesn't a scavenger hunt fit the bill?"

Rylee took another sip of her drink. Annie had valid points. And her suggestion wasn't corny at all. It just felt like a lot to pull together on short notice.

Annie leaned close and lowered her voice. "Heads up. This time I'm not joking. Sam's coming into the coffee shop and he's alone."

Oh, my. Determined not to let Sam catch her staring, she drained the last of her drink.

Stay. Calm. This is not a big deal.

The cold liquid did not do a single thing for the dryness in her throat. From behind the counter, the college student who worked for Annie offered a greeting, then turned on the grinder. Rylee set her empty cup aside and wiped her hands on her jeans. She couldn't *not* say hello. Sam paused near the bakery case and scanned the shop. When his gaze locked on hers, his mouth tipped up in a smile. Her pulse raced. She drew a steadying breath. The satisfying aroma of freshly ground coffee beans hung in the air.

"Wow," Annie murmured softly. "Girl, you're in so much trouble."

Rylee looked away from Sam just long enough to flash Annie her most exasperated look. "I am not," she murmured right before Sam arrived beside their table.

"Hi, ladies."

"Hi." Rylee managed to squeak out the word. Why was this happening? She'd spent plenty of time with Sam. His presence had never made her this nervous before.

Annie's knee bumped hers under the table in a pull-yourself-together nudge.

Rylee cleared her throat. "Have you met Annie Woodland?"

"Oh, yes. He's a frequent flyer around here." Annie pushed back her chair and stood. "Nice to see you again, Sam. What can I get started for you?"

"Hi, Annie." Sam tucked his hands in the back pockets of his jeans. "Regular coffee with cream, please."

"You got it." Annie tapped the back of her chair. "Have a seat. I'll be right back with your coffee."

"Thanks." Sam sat down across from Rylee.

Annie crossed the coffee shop and stepped behind the counter. Rylee shifted in her seat and tried not to notice the way his sweatshirt made his eyes look bluer than usual. Or the tousled strands of dark hair that dipped down on his forehead. "Where's Silas?"

"He's with his current babysitter," Sam said. "Hopefully, she'll last more than a day."

"Aww, I'm sorry to hear that you're struggling to find reliable childcare." Rylee pulled a face. "My sisters might have some more recommendations."

Sam pulled his phone from his pocket and checked the screen. "So far, so good. She seemed very confident with Silas, and her mom is hanging out in the lobby at the resort just in case there's an issue. What are you up to today?"

"Annie is helping me plan some wedding week festivities."

"More?"

"Yeah, that's what Annie said." Rylee pasted on a smile. "What do you think about a scavenger hunt?"

"Sounds intriguing." He dragged his hand across his face. "Forgive my lack of enthusiasm, but aren't there plenty of activities already?"

"Not according to the bride." Rylee wrinkled her nose. "I should've been the voice of reason and told her no, but I didn't, and here we are. I'm sorry."

"You don't have to apologize to me." Sam's phone buzzed in his hand. He glanced at the screen.

"Uh-oh. Babysitter?"

"Nope." He met her gaze and grinned. "An invitation for a Fourth of July flotilla. Now that's a prewedding festivity I fully support. Are you going?"

Rylee fumbled in her bag for her phone, retrieved it, and looked at the screen. A text from Crystal had arrived.

The Fourth of July flotilla is on! Josh's grandpa's boat at 9:00 a.m. Are you in?

She dropped her phone back in the bag without responding. "Sounds fun, but I'll have to check my schedule."

An expression she couldn't quite interpret flitted across Sam's face. "You're working on the Fourth?"

"Sometimes. It's good money."

"Here you go." Annie returned and set Sam's coffee in front of him, along with a plate of scones.

Sam smiled at her. "You didn't have to bring those."

"My treat." Annie gave Rylee a meaningful look. "Text me later."

"Of course."

To be honest, Rylee didn't want to miss the flotilla. And she did have to check in at work and make sure nothing had been added to her schedule. But mostly she had to be careful how much time she spent with Sam and Silas. The adorable little guy had won her over with his contagious belly laugh. But it wasn't wise to fall in love with her soon-to-be new boss. Given the way she'd responded just now to Sam's arrival at the coffee shop, it was time to double down. Fortify the walls around her heart. Because she'd been here before. Feeling smitten over a man who had no intention of sticking around. She wouldn't make the same mistake twice.

Chapter Seven

He'd been looking forward to this since he'd received the invitation.

Sam couldn't help but smile as he followed Josh and Crystal along the dock, his canvas sneakers thumping across the weathered boards. Thankfully, Silas remained fast asleep in his car seat. Sam had somehow managed to maneuver the contraption out of the car and into the stroller frame without waking the baby. Maybe he was getting the hang of this parenting thing.

Rylee trailed behind him with the backpack that doubled as his lifeline these days. The warm sun heated his skin. A pleasant breeze lifted his hair and carried the familiar tangy scent of salt.

"I cannot believe this weather." He glanced up at the cloudless sky. "What a gorgeous day."

"I know, right? Forecast originally called for rain," Rylee said. "This is the perfect day for a flotilla."

When Josh mentioned his grandfather had offered to participate in the Hearts Bay Fourth of July flotilla and invited Sam and Silas, Sam had said yes without a second thought. But then he'd remembered that he'd given his new baby-sitter the day off. She'd already had plans with her family to go out of town before she'd started working for him. So here he was, taking an infant on his first boat ride.

But he had to get used to folding Silas into all aspects of his life. If they were back in Seattle, they'd have at least one social activity to attend today. And he definitely wasn't going to give up boating. It had been such a big part of his life for as long as he could remember. Silas would gain his sea legs one way or another.

"I borrowed some sunscreen for sensitive skin from my sister Tess. Hope you don't mind. We need to put some on Silas's face."

We. Warmth unfurled in his chest at her word choice.

"Thanks for doing that. I guess that means he can't wear the same stuff as adults?"

"He probably can, but since he's a sensitive fella, I made sure to get the lotion kind and not the spray."

"Oh, of course."

He tried to pretend he was following her train of thought. To be honest, he hadn't packed any sunscreen. For himself or Silas. What would he do without Rylee to remind him of all the details he'd overlooked?

When he'd run into Rylee at The Trading Post yesterday, she hadn't seemed thrilled about the flotilla. So he'd been pleasantly surprised when he'd gotten her text last night saying that she'd be there. In the privacy of his suite, he'd pumped his fist in the air.

"There she is," Josh said, stopping beside a boat slip with an impressive 26-foot cabin cruiser named *Summer Lovin'* bobbing in the green-blue water. A man with a salt-and-pepper beard, a gray bucket-style hat on his head, and a red-plaid button-down layered over a gray T-shirt waved from the back deck. He wiped his hands on his faded jeans, then stepped closer.

"Welcome them on board, Joshie. So glad you guys could make it. Happy Fourth of July!"

Sam chuckled at the man's nickname for Josh. He'd have to tease him about that later.

"I'm Captain Henry." His voice carried a gravelly tone. "Come on now. Don't be shy."

Crystal and Josh led the way, stepping carefully from the dock onto the boat's fiberglass deck. Sam stood on the dock, uncertain how to proceed with the stroller.

"Oh, what do we have here? A young sailor." Captain Henry's friendly smile didn't falter as he eyed Silas in the car seat.

"Hope you don't mind, sir, if I bring a baby on board?"

"Not a problem, son. I've had my fair share of youngsters along for the ride over the years. Joshie here took his first ride probably when he was in his mother's tummy."

"Not on this boat, Grandpa." Josh lifted the lid on the cooler and retrieved two cans of soda. He handed one to Crystal.

"No, no. Had a much different vessel back then. Joshie, help him get that stroller on board, will you? Make yourselves comfortable. Got water and soda in the cooler. We'll be under-way in just a few minutes." Captain Henry adjusted his hat and stepped inside the cabin.

Sam gently detached the car seat from the stroller. Silas stirred but didn't wake up.

Rylee lowered the bag to the dock, deftly collapsed the stroller and handed it to Josh.

"Thanks," Sam said, offering her a grateful smile.

"No problem," Rylee said.

He carefully boarded the boat, set the car seat

at his feet, then turned around and extended his hand to Rylee.

"Thank you." She smiled, her fingers warm as she clasped his hand. She stepped onto the deck beside him. The boat dipped and swayed, adjusting to the addition of four more adults and a baby.

Sam squeezed her hand and held on for a second longer than necessary. Two appealing splotches of color blossomed on her face. Her gaze flitted away and she slipped her hand from his. Drat. He'd been hoping to hold on a little longer, even though he had no right to do so.

Friends. You're just friends.

Except he was starting to want so much more. She was funny and pretty and so very smart. They employed women at Frazier Aviation who were exceptional pilots, but he'd never met anyone quite like Rylee. An ache filled his chest at the thought of going back to Seattle before the end of the month. He wasn't ready to say goodbye. But a new dating relationship right now felt reckless. The timing was the worst.

He claimed a spot on the cushioned bench seat at the back of the boat. Rylee sat beside him. He gently slid Silas's car seat closer. The baby stirred, his little forehead scrunching with annoyance. Sam froze.

"Here." Rylee retrieved the pacifier from its

spot tucked in beside Silas's legs, then popped it in his mouth. They both stared. Waiting.

"Please don't wake up," Sam whispered. They hadn't even pulled away from the dock yet.

Silas's little mouth began sucking, jostling the pacifier. His eyes remained closed.

Sam blew out a relieved breath and quietly high-fived Rylee. "What do you think? Will he sleep the entire time?"

"Probably not." She bumped his shoulder with hers. "But I admire your optimistic outlook. Have you ever taken a baby on a boat ride before?"

"Nope."

"Huh. Well, maybe Silas will be a huge fan."

She could not have been more wrong about Silas and his attitude toward a boat ride.

As soon as Henry started the engines and eased away from the dock, Silas jolted awake and burst into tears.

A muscle in Sam's cheek twitched.

Rylee exchanged nervous glances with Crystal.

Sam blew out a breath, then leaned down and unfastened the buckles on Silas's five-point harness.

"Do you want me to hold him?" Rylee offered.

"Is he hungry or thirsty?" Crystal removed her sunglasses from the top of her head and slid them onto her face. "Maybe he needs a diaper change."

Sam gently scooped the crying baby into his arms. Poor guy. He looked so frazzled. Silas's body trembled as he screamed. Tears slid down his flushed cheeks as his face turned an alarming shade of deep red.

"Whoa. He's really getting worked up," Josh said. "How can we help?"

Sam smoothed his hand over Silas's hair. It clung to his forehead, dampened with sweat.

"We need to put his life jacket on." Sam awkwardly nestled Silas in the crook of his elbow.

"If that's what you think is best." Rylee peeked inside Sam's bag. "Where is it?"

"I—I don't know." Sam leveled her with his gaze. "Didn't you put his life jacket in the bottom of the stroller?"

His tone made her wince. She swallowed back a blunt reply. Sam hadn't asked her to put anything in the bottom of the stroller. Her job had been to carry the bag down the dock. "Would you like me to hold Silas while you look for the life jacket?"

"I'll look for an extra life jacket." Josh stood and moved toward the boat's cabin. "Grandpa always has plenty."

"Thanks." Sam tried to sway side to side but with the boat's gentle bobbing on the water, he ended up stumbling.

Rylee reached out to steady him. His skin was warm under her fingers and the corded muscles in his forearm hinted at his strength. "Would you like to sit down? Maybe we can try giving him a bottle?"

Sam nodded and sank onto the nearest bench seat. She linked her arms across her chest. Surely there was something they could do to help Silas calm down. She hadn't seen him this worked up since they'd met. A band set up at the edge of the refueling dock nearby broke into the opening notes of a patriotic song. Two dogs standing on the bow of a sailboat tied off in a slip started barking.

Silas's cries had taken on a different tone. Raw. Desperate. Rylee wanted to climb right out of her skin. "Sam, I think he's scared."

Sam's face turned pale. "I don't know what to do other than get off the boat."

Rylee turned and gave Crystal a you've-got-to-help-us glance. Captain Henry turned from his position at the wheel. "Anything you need?"

"I hate to ask this, but I think we might have to go back," Rylee said, raising her voice so he could hear her above all the racket.

"Go back?" Henry frowned, then shook his

head. "Not yet. We're just getting started. He'll be all right. Fresh air and sunshine do a body good."

Oh, no. Rylee sat down beside Sam and looked around. They were seventh or eighth in a long line of boats, easing their way out of the marina toward the bay surrounding the island. Captain Henry was right. They couldn't exit the flotilla until they passed the buoys marking the no-wake zone. With boats behind and in front of them, there really wasn't anywhere else for Henry to go.

"Here." Josh returned from down below with a small pale blue life jacket. "Try this. We've had it forever but it will keep him safe."

Rylee pressed her lips into a flat line. Silas would hate wearing the thing.

"Did you happen to bring a hat?" Crystal asked. "Maybe the sun is too bright."

"No hat." Sam was clearly irritated.

"Let me hold him." Rylee stretched out her arms. "Do you have formula?"

"I've got one bottle mixed already, but I just fed him."

"Maybe it will comfort him," Rylee said.

Sam handed Silas over. "You're right. It's worth a try."

"Come here, sweet boy." Rylee braced Silas

against her shoulder. He arched his back, resisting her. "Oh, my."

Silas looked up at her. His cries wracked his little body.

"I know. You're miserable. We're trying to get this figured out." Rylee pressed a kiss to his hot forehead.

The boat rocked and swayed as they rode over the wake of the boat in front of them. Humming softly, she tried pulling him closer. He was not having it. Silas screamed louder and tried twisting out of her embrace.

Josh stood and placed his hand on his grandfather's arm. "We're going to have to take them back. That kid just will not stop crying."

Henry turned and offered an empathetic glance. "Yeah, I suppose you're right. Poor little fella. Just can't get happy, can he? I'll figure out how to get back to the dock. We'll be swimming upstream for a few minutes."

"You hear that, little buddy?" Rylee shifted Silas to her other shoulder and patted his back gently. "We're going to help you. You're going to be all right."

Silas squinted against the sunlight as they picked up speed. Strands of her hair blew across his face.

"Oh, sorry about that." Rylee freed her hair from Silas's face. He kept wailing, clutching her shirtsleeve in his fist. Surely he'd stop crying soon.

Red-white-and-blue banners streamed from the masts of boats. An American flag mounted on Henry's bow snapped in the breeze. Seagulls soared overhead. It really was too bad that he couldn't calm down. The flotilla was a great tradition. She hadn't always wanted to participate after Charlie and Abner had passed, but she'd rallied, put her lingering grief aside, and agreed to ride along today for Sam and Silas's sake.

Sam handed her a full bottle of formula. "Let's see if he'll drink this."

She nodded, then took the bottle and gently settled Silas on her lap. He spotted the bottle and screamed louder, shoving it away with his hand.

Dread pitted her stomach. She handed the bottle back. "What do you want to do now?"

Sam heaved a defeated sigh. "I don't know. I'm really sorry. We should've stayed at the resort."

"Nonsense." Rylee switched Silas to her other shoulder. "The day isn't over yet. You'll see. We'll end this one on a high note, I promise."

Rylee had made good on her promise.

Sam stood in her family's backyard. The Maddens' Fourth of July party was not at all what he'd expected. Somehow he'd envisioned Rylee's siblings, their spouses and kids. The usual holiday cookout menu of hamburgers and hot dogs, and maybe some brownies and ice cream for dessert. Instead, there had to be over a hundred people gathered. Had the whole town turned out for this?

Tiki torches staked in the ground at various intervals around the perimeter of the property burned bright in a desperate attempt to keep the mosquitoes away. The evening sun crept toward the mountains, spilling its golden rays across the emerald-green water of the bay. Sam tipped his head back and admired the wispy clouds edged with shades of pink. Coral and orange streaks like brushstrokes swept across a pale blue canvas, creating the perfect canopy for their holiday celebration.

Folks clustered in small groups across the lush green lawn. Kids bounced on the trampoline in front of a smaller house nestled in the woods. An impressive fire blazed in a pit, orange and red flames licking the wood. Children and adults ringed the fire, holding sticks freshly whittled from the willow trees nearby. Marshmallows on those sticks hovered over the flames and the sweet aroma of melted sugar hung in the air.

Rylee made her way across the lawn. Their

eyes met and his pulse quickened. She wore a red V-necked sweater, jeans that flared at the bottom and white sneakers. She must've done something different with her hair because loose curls bounced against her slender shoulders as she walked toward him.

"Hey, Sam." She stopped beside him and smiled. "Are you having a good time?"

"The best Fourth of July party I've seen in quite some time." He grinned and took a sip of his soda.

"Wow, that's high praise." She turned and surveyed the crowd. "My parents love hosting this party every year. It's become one of our favorite traditions."

"Did you happen to see Silas when you were inside?"

"Oh, yes." Rylee turned back to face him. "He's having the time of his life. Mia's holding him and all the ladies are gathered around, fawning over his long dark eyelashes. It's safe to say he's the life of the party."

"Oh, good." Relief left his lips with a gusty breath. "After that boat ride today, I wasn't sure he'd ever smile again."

"Did he take a long nap this afternoon?"

"Three hours and fifteen minutes." Sam punched the air with his fist. "I savored every single minute of silence."

Rylee's smile turned empathetic. "That poor little fella. He must've been worn out."

"Yeah, that makes two of us. Should I offer to buy Captain Henry lunch at The Tide Pool or something? I feel awful about how that all went down."

She offered a dismissive wave. "Don't worry about it. He's probably had cantankerous passengers on board before."

"But they had to leave the flotilla because of me."

Rylee pressed her hand against his forearm. A pleasant warmth zinged along his arm and bloomed in his chest.

"Sam, Silas was overwhelmed and probably afraid. You couldn't have known he'd react that way. So don't be so hard on yourself."

He looked down and nudged a pine cone on the ground with the toe of his sneaker. "I just hate that we messed up their plans."

"You didn't mess up anything. After we got off the boat, Josh, Crystal and Henry went right back out on the water. I saw her posts on social media. They had a fantastic time."

"Well, great. Now I'm jealous that I missed it."

Rylee laughed. A sweet musical sound that he could definitely get used to hearing.

"Come on." She gestured over her shoulder. "Let's go get some food before it's gone."

They walked side by side, weaving their way through the people clustered on the lawn, spread out on blankets and sitting in circles in their canvas chairs.

"What did you do while Silas slept? Did you take a nap too?"

Sam hesitated, letting Rylee go in front of him. They joined the line of folks waiting patiently to fill their plates. The Maddens had put out an abundant spread across two long tables pushed against the wall of their house. Popular country music streamed from a wireless speaker. The hum of conversation and children's laughter filled the air.

He took the plate Rylee offered him. "I took about a twenty-minute nap. Then a friend of mine in Nicaragua called me on FaceTime with an update."

Rylee's eyes widened. "An update? Are you acquiring a company in Nicaragua?"

"Not exactly," Sam said. "We're looking into digging more wells so people can have clean drinking water."

She set her plate on the table and gently split her hamburger bun open on her plate. "Oh, that's right. You'd mentioned that that was one of your passion projects."

"It's my main passion project, to be honest. As soon as this acquisition is all straightened out, I plan to make fundraising and clean water access my day job."

Rylee studied him, the tongs holding her hamburger halfway to her plate. "So once the merger is final, who will be appointed the general manager here?"

He hesitated before adding a bun and a hot dog to his plate. "That's an excellent question. I hate that I don't have an answer."

"Good to know," Rylee said, avoiding his gaze as she layered the patty onto the bun. "You've already admitted you're not that into planes. I assumed you'd been sent here to act on behalf of your family."

"I'm here to oversee the due diligence process and share crucial information with the board of directors. I doubt that they'll accept my input regarding staffing recommendations."

"Why not?"

He paused. How much should he share about the complicated dynamics of disappointing his father by leaving the family business? "Even before my brother and sister-in-law's accident, I had planned to resign. That's created some… tension. To be honest, my father doesn't seem to understand that sometimes I can hardly sleep at night knowing that there are people in the world who can't have clean water to drink."

Rylee glanced up at him. Was that admiration in her eyes? He couldn't tell.

"Have you always been concerned about humanitarian relief?"

"Great question." Sam added mustard, relish and ketchup to his hot dog. "I wish I could tell you that I've always cared about the needs of others, but it wasn't until recently that I really started to pay attention. I heard someone speak at a fundraising event in Seattle two years ago and, afterward, we spoke for a few minutes. He invited me to get involved with his foundation. I was too afraid at the time to tell my parents I didn't want to be involved in the family business anymore, but the lack of clean water didn't seem like a problem I could keep ignoring."

"Makes sense." Rylee added a scoop of pasta salad and some fresh fruit to her plate, then politely waited while Sam did the same.

A few minutes later, they found two empty chairs and sat beside Tess, Asher and their daughter Lucy.

Conversation ebbed and flowed as Sam tucked into his meal. He was glad he'd told Rylee more about his future plans, but doubt crept in, niggling at him as he watched the kids play with their sparklers. Later, when fireworks burst across the pale blue sky overhead, Sam longed to reach out and clasp Rylee's hand in his own. He quickly tamped the thought down and fisted his hands in his lap. His time in Hearts Bay was ending. Before long, he and Silas would be on their way back to Seattle. Back to his bachelor pad and finding a new normal.

Back to his comfortable world that sorely lacked one key feature—someone to share his life with.

"I put away the leftover pasta salad," Annie said, pulling the back door closed as she stepped into the backyard. "Here are the maps and directions for tomorrow. I've...uh-oh. What's wrong?"

"Nothing." Rylee shook her head, then turned away and grabbed the last bag of garbage Gus had collected from the container stationed near the fire pit.

"Did something happen with Sam?" Annie fell in step beside her as Rylee carted the bag to the larger bins beside her parents' garage. "You guys looked like you were having a nice time together."

Yeah, that's the problem. "I'm fine, Annie. Nothing happened."

Annie stepped into her path. Determination hardened her expression. "I've been your friend for a bazillion years, and you only do that thing with your mouth when you're about to get upset."

So much for keeping her feelings under wraps. "What thing with my mouth?"

"This." Annie puffed out her cheeks and quirked her lips to one side.

Rylee rolled her eyes, tightened her grip on the bag and sidestepped Annie. "I do not make that face."

"Yes, you do. Ask anyone who loves you and they'll tell you it's true." The brown paper package Annie held crinkled as she followed Rylee to the trash bins. "Now, would you please pause the party cleanup for two seconds and tell me what's going on?"

Rylee clamped her mouth shut, hurled the bag into the container and shoved the lid closed. "Okay, you're right, something did happen, but I still don't think I make that face."

Annie bit her lip, then lifted her eyes heavenward.

"What are you doing?"

"Praying."

Rylee frowned. "Right now?"

"Yes, because you are jumping on my last nerve. Would you please let me help you? It's almost one o'clock in the morning and I have to be up in five hours to open the shop."

"All right, all right." Rylee held up her hand. "I'm sorry. I didn't mean to make this difficult."

Annie's countenance softened. "It's okay. Just give me the scoop and then we can both go to bed."

Rylee stole a quick glance around the yard. Only her family members and Annie remained. The last of the party guests had gone home about thirty minutes ago. A tendril of smoke from the coals still burning in the fire pit curled into the air. Gus and Mia had rounded up the last of the stray plastic cups abandoned on the lawn. Dad and Mom had put away the tables and chairs, then gone inside to check on their grandkids, who'd fallen asleep on the living room floor watching a movie. Man, she loved this party. These people. The way their community gathered to celebrate Independence Day. She couldn't imagine living anywhere else.

"Rylee?" Annie touched her arm. "You don't have to tell me anything you don't want to."

"It's not that I don't want to tell you. This isn't scandalous news or anything. I'm just embarrassed about my feelings." Rylee let her voice drop to a whisper. Oh, why was this so hard? Annie had been one of her closest friends for eons. Clearly, she cared or she wouldn't have persisted. Rylee looked down and jabbed at a pebble on the concrete with the toe of her shoe. "Sam has mentioned more than once that he's passionate about clean water access in developing countries. Nicaragua, for example."

"Well, that's cool," Annie said.

"Oh, for sure, except he's not going to work for Frazier Aviation much longer. As soon as the merger goes through, he's resigning so he can focus on his fundraising and humanitarian work."

"That's a big change, especially since he has Silas to think about." Annie tucked a strand of hair behind her ear. "Are you worried about keeping your job?"

Rylee nodded, blinking back unexpected tears. Oh, brother. Why was she coming undone over this? "I was hoping he'd have some say in who would be the new general manager or make staffing recommendations if they decide to cut jobs."

"Did he tell you your job was in danger?"

Rylee shook her head.

"Is Carson worried he might lose his?"

Rylee lifted one shoulder. "I—I don't know. Didn't ask. But part of me still hoped Sam would advocate for me."

Annie's brow furrowed.

"I know what you're going to say." Rylee sniffed. "That I should have faith and trust in

God's provision, and that everything happens for a reason—"

"Frankly, I wasn't planning on leading with that, although everything you just said is true."

Rylee swallowed against the tight ache in her throat. "I've worked so hard to get where I am. What if I have to move? I don't want to start over with another airline in Anchorage or Fairbanks. This is my home."

"Oh, Rylee." Annie's eyes gleamed with unshed tears. "You're not wrong for being concerned. Paul and Libby selling their business is a huge deal. Feelings matter and yours are valid."

It seemed like Annie had more she wanted to add. "But…"

"The bigger issue is that you're worried he doesn't care about you, and that's super painful."

Oh.

"You're worth caring about, Rylee. I don't know if Sam's the one for you, but if he is, you'll know because he won't let wells in Nicaragua or mergers and acquisitions or being a single dad get in the way."

This time, Rylee couldn't hold back her tears. "I want to believe you."

Annie set the package aside then pulled her in for a hug. "I'm sorry that you're hurting. Maybe not today or even tomorrow, but I hope one day soon you'll find the courage to let someone see and love the real you."

Wow, that stung. She had not been prepared for Annie's spot-on observations. Worse, she didn't know how to move forward. Yes, she wanted very much to keep her job. But Annie was right. The deepest longing of her heart was to love a man who'd love *her* enough to stay.

Chapter Eight

"Sam, you don't have to help." Rylee sat down on the leather couch in the lobby of the resort. "I can handle giving the guests the maps and instructions."

Wow, she was stubborn. "Can you hold him for me, please?"

"Absolutely."

Sam gently lowered Silas onto Rylee's lap. The baby squealed and kicked his legs, rewarding Rylee with a slobbery grin.

Her radiant smile and the affection she showered on Silas drew a few appreciative glances from guests passing through the lobby.

Huh. Sam paused, mesmerized by Rylee's ability to provoke Silas's heartwarming belly laugh. She caught him staring and held his gaze just long enough to make his cheeks flush.

He turned away and fiddled with the bouncy

seat he'd set on the floor beside the couch. Then he pawed through his ever-present diaper bag, pretending to inventory its contents. As if he were that organized. Most of the time he couldn't find what he was looking for in that thing. Setting the bag at his feet, he sat on the leather couch opposite Rylee. A rustic wooden coffee table with a faux floral centerpiece filled the space between them. Sam surveyed the impressive piece of furniture. Thankfully, Silas wasn't mobile yet. Those corners looked dangerous.

He couldn't help but smile. Three weeks ago, thoughts like that would've never entered his mind.

"Did you hear what I said? You don't have to stay. I've got this."

Rylee held Silas and bounced her knee up and down. Silas's coos grew louder. She bounced her knee faster until he squealed again.

Sam chuckled. The boy clearly loved the attention. He had one finger jammed in the side of his mouth and he stared at Rylee like she was the source of all happiness.

"I heard what you said, but I still to want to help. You've already done too much for Josh and Crystal. There's no reason why you need to supervise the scavenger hunt too."

"I'm handing out maps and giving people instructions. It's not that hard."

"Perfect." Sam rubbed his palms together. "Then you won't mind if I hang out and give you a hand."

"But you have Silas to think about. Isn't he missing his morning nap?"

"He's in a good mood right now and doesn't seem sleepy to me. Probably because he slept in this morning."

Okay, so only thirty minutes later than normal, but it still counted. Besides, he wasn't backing down. There was no way he was going to sit upstairs in his suite while Rylee spent her morning here in the lobby handing out instructions and maps and whatever else Josh and Crystal had persuaded her to do. As best man, he should help with these activities.

She eyed him with a doubtful look. "Okay, but the second he gets grumpy, I want you to take him back upstairs."

"You are not good at accepting help, are you?"

A pained expression flitted across her face. "Not really."

Drat. Sam scrubbed his fingers along his jaw. Maybe he shouldn't have said that.

Silas grabbed at Rylee's necklace and tugged. "Oh, easy there, big guy." She gently extracted the pendant from his pudgy fist, then tucked it out of sight underneath the collar of her T-shirt. Silas fussed in protest. She turned him around so he faced Sam instead. Boy, she was really good at defusing a crisis.

"Where are these maps and when can we expect our first guests?"

Rylee pulled a large manila envelope from her tote bag and handed it over. "Maps are inside. We're expecting twenty guests to stop by between ten and ten thirty."

He carefully extracted the papers and scanned the top page. "Wow, this is beautiful."

The hand-drawn illustration of the island featured landmarks, appealing graphics and a playful color scheme.

"It's supposed to double as a map for today's scavenger hunt and a memorable souvenir," Rylee said.

"Did you hire someone to design this?"

"Let's just say I had to call in a favor or three to make this happen."

Sam set the stack of maps on the coffee table. He didn't like the sound of that. Not at all. "What do you mean?"

"Between getting the local artists to design and draw the map, and collecting the glass floats that everyone will be looking for today, I'll be cleaning Annie's bathrooms at the coffee shop and taking the graphic designer and her whole family for a flightseeing trip soon."

Frowning, Sam glanced at her. "Why do you have to clean Annie's bathrooms?"

"Because the scavenger hunt was her idea. I went to her, begging for help at the last minute. She got the glass floats donated from an artist friend."

"I see." Sam leaned back on the sofa. His scalp prickled. "Josh and Crystal have relied on you for too much. I should be helping more."

"You have Silas to look after, and I'm capable of pitching in."

"You've been at every wedding-related activity, worked full-time, filled in for Paul and Libby, and helped me out whenever I've had trouble with Silas." Sam leaned forward and braced his elbows on his knees. "You must be exhausted."

"Crystal and I have been friends for years. I'm going to push through and make sure her wedding is incredibly special. Don't worry. I have plenty of vacation. I'll be sure to take time off soon."

"When?"

"Soon." She smiled but he wasn't fooled. Exhaustion swam in her eyes. "Here are our first scavenger hunt participants."

Sam turned and followed her gaze toward the

resort's entrance. The vaulted ceiling, rough-hewn logs and the impressive moose with antlers mounted on the wall really made the resort feel like an authentic Alaskan outpost. The food had been incredible and the staff accommodating to all his needs with Silas. And now they were graciously welcoming several of Josh and Crystal's out-of-town guests and the rest of the wedding party.

Rylee stood, shifted Silas to her hip, then greeted the couple with elementary-aged children, a boy and a girl. "Hi there. Are you here for Josh and Crystal's scavenger hunt?"

The woman smiled, her strawberry blonde ponytail swishing against the fabric of her green vest. "Yes we are. I'm Nina and this is my husband, Jaden. We are so excited!"

"That's awesome. Welcome to Hearts Bay. It's nice to meet you," Rylee said. "I'm Rylee, the maid of honor, and this is my little buddy, Silas. This is Sam, Josh's best man."

"How's it going?" Sam smiled and gave a polite nod. "We have a map here for you and some basic instructions."

Rylee handed Nina a half sheet of paper. Sam passed the map to the boy. His sister leaned in to peek over his shoulder.

"My phone number is on the bottom of the

instructions," Rylee said. "Text me if you need anything."

"This is going to be so fun." The woman bounced up on her toes and glanced at her husband. The guy still hadn't said a word. He frowned and clutched his to-go cup of coffee, his baseball cap pulled low over his eyes.

Rylee ignored him. "I hope you all have a wonderful time."

After the family left, Rylee turned back toward the couch. Silas's expression crumpled and he started to cry.

"You don't have to keep holding him. He'll be fine in his bouncy seat," Sam said.

"All right." Rylee carefully lowered him into the contraption and buckled the plastic clips to keep him secure. Silas kicked his legs and cooed at her, making the small gray-and-white chair bounce.

She patted his leg. "Enjoy."

Yawning, she reclaimed her seat on the couch.

"When I came down here for breakfast this morning, a man had put rose petals all over the floor leading from the buffet to a table by the windows." Sam gestured to the dining area on the other side of the building. "He had this gorgeous arrangement of flowers waiting too. The staff said he and his wife are here celebrating their fiftieth wedding anniversary."

"We're fond of love here in Hearts Bay." Rylee pulled a water bottle from her tote bag and twisted off the cap. "I never imagined we'd become such a destination wedding kind of place."

"Is it true that heart-shaped rocks wash up on shore?"

Rylee took a sip of water, then put the cap back on. "The heart-shaped rocks at the edge of the bay are our most popular landmark. Occasionally someone finds a smaller heart-shaped rock on the beach."

"Have you?"

"Not yet. My nephew Cameron likes to look for them out by my parents' place."

"Does the winner of the scavenger hunt win anything heart-shaped?" Sam asked.

Rylee's water bottle crinkled in her hand. "Good question. I'm sure you'll find this hard to believe, but I outsourced that part to Chelsea. She gets to oversee the prizes. People will get to keep the glass floats when they find them."

"That's cool." Sam checked on Silas. His eyelids were getting heavy. Maybe the little guy needed a nap after all.

He sank back on the couch cushions. "What's the most romantic thing anyone's ever done for you?"

She shot him a perplexed look. "Why are you asking?"

"Because we're talking about Hearts Bay, destination weddings, and our friends are marrying each other in three days. I'm just making conversation."

She frowned. "I don't have an answer."

"Oh, come on. No singing telegrams from high school boyfriends? Or promposals spelled out in rose petals on your lawn? Wait. I know." He held up his hand. "Somebody dedicated a song to you on the radio?"

She rolled her eyes. "How corny. No, thank you. Next, you'll be asking me if I have any old mixtapes."

"Do you?"

"Nope."

An awkward silence hovered over them. Sam shifted on the couch. "So you're not going to answer my question?"

"I told you, I don't have a sweet swoonworthy story. Sadly, my last boyfriend ran off with my cousin. They live in Texas now."

Ouch. Sam rubbed his palm against his chest. "That hurts."

"Tell me about it."

"I'm so sorry."

She shrugged. "It happens. Better to find out

before we were engaged that he wasn't interested in being faithful."

"Were you about to be engaged?"

"I thought so." Pain pinched her features. "I should've known better anyway."

"What do you mean?"

"He wasn't from here. Just passing through on a fishing trip with his buddies. I should have known better than to fall for someone who'd never stay."

Sam's breath locked in his lungs. Is that what she thought of him too? An outsider who'd never stay?

Rylee's phone hummed. She glanced at the screen. "I'm going to step outside and take this call. Will you pass out the maps and instructions?"

He swallowed hard. Managed a quick nod. Wow, he'd been foolish. Misinterpreted their entire conversation. And apparently every other interaction they'd had. He thought they'd shared a moment. He'd even been flirting. At least a little bit. But she clearly didn't see him that way. Good thing he'd stumbled across the truth. Somehow he'd have to find a way to convince his heart she wasn't for him.

If she'd painted her own fingernails, she'd be done by now. Instead, her manicure, courtesy of Lexi, was taking three times as long. Worse, Mia and Tess had asked no less than twenty-seven questions and they'd only been together for an hour. If only her sister Eliana were here. She'd sideline their inquisition with a funny story about Willow or Hunter.

"You're going to need a second coat." Lexi twisted the cap for the pink nail polish back on and set the bottle aside. "Then I'll add this amazing topcoat. You'll love it. The polish won't chip for at least five days."

"Great."

Lexi narrowed her gaze. "What's wrong?"

"Nothing." Rylee lifted one shoulder. "Just ready to be finished."

"With the manicure or this wedding?"

"Both."

"Did you take this week off from work?" Tess carried a bowl of popcorn into Mia's family room.

Rylee shook her head. "I was supposed to take Sam on a flightseeing trip today, but the weather was questionable so we rescheduled."

"Is the flightseeing trip necessary for the acquisition?" Mia sat on her sofa with the remote control in her hand. They were supposed to be watching a movie, but so far all they'd done was talk about the wedding.

"Frazier Aviation's board of directors requested that Sam observe all aspects of the business," Rylee said. "Since flightseeing is a large part of what we do, it makes sense that he would take at least one trip while he's here."

"You should take him out to see Grandmother." Tess popped the top on a can of soda. "Then he can have an authentic Orca Island experience."

"That was my plan, but the weather didn't cooperate." Rylee glanced out the window. Rain pelted Gus and Mia's windows and ribbons of fog wound through the trees in their front yard.

Poppy's squeals of delight filtered down the hall. Gus had convinced Poppy to play a game of hide-and-seek instead of getting her fingernails painted. He'd volunteered to handle her bedtime routine, so Rylee and her sisters could get their movie started, but things were moving slowly.

Rylee stifled a yawn with her hand.

"Whoa, don't mess up your new polish," Lexi said. "I know you don't want me to have to start over."

"I sure don't."

The sooner she got out of here, the better. She obediently splayed her hands flat on Lexi's dining room table. An ache throbbed behind her eyes. How long did her nails have to dry before she could crawl into bed?

Lexi's kind eyes filled with concern. "Are you all right?"

"I'm fine." She forced a smile. "Exhausted. That's all."

Lexi quirked her mouth to one side and uncapped the nail polish.

Rylee'd tossed and turned last night, replaying yesterday's conversation with Sam in the lobby of the resort. Had he been flirting with her? She couldn't be sure. At her parents' Fourth of July party, they'd most definitely had a moment. And then when he'd brought up romantic grand gestures, she'd been quite honest.

Maybe a little too honest. But that didn't change the facts. She couldn't fall in love with someone like Sam. He had huge aspirations. A generous, philanthropic heart. And a six-month-old relying on him for the rest of his life.

There wasn't room for her in that crowded equation.

"How are things going with Sam and Silas?" Lexi swiped the brush across Rylee's index finger in three deliberate strokes. "He's a brave guy, traveling here with a baby. Did he get his childcare issues sorted out?"

Rylee measured her words carefully. Lexi didn't have a mean bone in her body. She was only asking out of genuine concern. But Rylee wasn't interested in breaking down how things were going with Sam. Because they weren't going anywhere. A relationship with him was like navigating a flight approach that ran out of runway. She desperately needed an evasive maneuver.

"Rylee?"

Mia's voice pulled her back to the conversation.

"Huh?" Rylee blinked and glanced from Mia to Lexi and then to Tess. They all wore puzzled expressions.

"Did Sam find childcare for the rehearsal dinner?" Tess scooped popcorn into a small bowl and passed it to Mia. "Asher and I can watch Silas if he doesn't find someone."

"Thanks for the offer, but he has babysitters lined up for the rest of the week. Silas is doing better now that he's drinking that special formula."

Mia picked a classic nineties rom-com and pressed Play. The familiar opening scene filled the television screen.

"He's a nice guy," Lexi said. "I enjoyed chatting with him when he came by for dinner at our place last week."

"He is nice," Rylee agreed. "Very kind. If he ever gets married, he'll make a great husband."

Lexi glanced up, wide-eyed. "Is there a reason why he wouldn't get married?"

"I don't know if he's opposed to marriage. He hasn't said. But when he talks about his future, he sounds more concerned with taking care of Silas and philanthropy than finding a wife."

"So more of a confirmed bachelor then?" Lexi shifted her focus back to painting Rylee's nails.

Rylee groaned. "I—I don't know. Forget I said anything. Sam gave me kind of a strange vibe the other night at the Fourth of July thing, but I think it was all in my head."

"Say more." Lexi dragged the wet brush slowly down the center of Rylee's ring finger. "What do you mean by 'strange vibe'?"

"He kept looking at me like maybe he might kiss me." Warmth heated her skin. "It might've been the fireworks and wishful thinking."

"Did he say anything else about it?" Lexi asked. "You've seen him since then, right?"

"We were at the resort yesterday, handing out maps for the scavenger hunt, and the conversation took an odd turn. He asked me if anyone had ever done anything super romantic for me. I told him about how my last boyfriend fell in love with my cousin and left town and…now I'm feeling flustered and not sure what to say."

"Aww, that's sweet." Lexi smiled. "He wants to know your love language."

Rylee scrunched up her nose. "My love language?"

"You know, do you like to receive gifts from your significant other? Or would you prefer words of affirmation?" Lexi dipped the brush back inside the bottle. "Hang with me, I'm almost finished here."

"He looked at me like I'd kind of wounded him. And now I wonder if I said too much." Rylee tipped back her head and groaned. "Why am I so bad at this?"

Mia held up the remote and paused the movie. "Whoa, there's a lot to unpack there."

"Mia," Tess said, clearly exasperated. "We didn't even make it three minutes. What are you doing?"

"This conversation that Lexi and Rylee are having is way more interesting." Mia pulled her legs up and tucked them underneath her. "All right, spill."

"I literally just told you everything." Rylee glared at Mia. "And did I mention that I'm exhausted?"

"Not that you asked, but it's obvious to me that you both like each other. I saw the way you were talking and laughing at the Fourth of July party. He's into you."

"Doesn't matter," Rylee said. "He's leaving the island after the wedding."

"How long after the wedding?" Lexi asked. "A few days? A week?"

"Come on, Rylee," Tess said. "Take a risk. Put yourself out there. Let him know how you feel."

Anger flared in her abdomen. "You cannot be serious."

Tess, Lexi and Mia exchanged confused looks. "Why not?"

Rylee opened her mouth to protest, then closed it, then opened it again. "I don't know why I'm trying to explain myself to the three of you. You're all happily married with children."

This time, Tess looked wounded. "What's that supposed to mean?"

"It means you're settled. Secure. Happy. You've already forgotten how hard it is because you all have what you wanted. Everything worked out for you."

Lexi gasped.

Rylee winced. Okay, so maybe that last part was a bit insensitive. Still, she pressed on. Emotion made her throat ache. "I just need you to acknowledge that not everybody gets to have their happily-ever-after."

"We're well aware, Rylee," Mia said softly.

"Just…never mind." She pulled her hand away. "Thanks, Lexi. I need to go."

Shoving back her chair, she grabbed her coat and her purse and hurried to the door.

"Wait, don't go," Tess called after her. "Let's talk about this."

"See you." Rylee shoved her feet into her shoes and stepped out into the pouring rain. As she hurried to her car, she let the tears fall. Why didn't her sisters understand? Not everyone had the courage to put themselves out there again.

Chapter Nine

The next time someone invited her to be the maid of honor at a wedding, she'd think twice before saying yes.

Rylee's vision of the role and Crystal's expectations had not exactly aligned. Rylee fished two ibuprofen tablets from the container inside her purse and downed them along with a sip of ice water. Eating a meal at Hank's had always been a treat. Too bad she wasn't in the mood to enjoy it.

Across the table, Sam caught her eye. Light from the burning candles in the black lanterns at the center of the table flickered across his clean-shaven jaw. He raised his eyebrows. She put down her glass, formed her mouth into a polite smile and pretended she didn't notice the concern in his lingering gaze.

The servers paraded in, cleared the salad

and appetizer plates and then refilled their drinks. Chelsea's obnoxious laughter punctuated the air. Rylee groaned inwardly. If only she'd arrived at the restaurant earlier. Then she might've had time to rearrange the name tags or something. Given the opportunity, she would've put some distance between her place at the table and Chelsea's.

And she never would've sat so close to Sam.

She zipped her purse closed and hooked it to the back of her chair. The fragrant aroma of marinara and garlic permeated the room. Resisting the urge to check the time on her watch, she rearranged her cloth napkin on her lap. She'd devoured her salad and had more than enough of the appetizers that had been passed around. The power bar and fruit smoothie she'd consumed on the go for lunch had long since evaporated. Today had been hectic, helping Crystal and Josh and their families get ready for the rehearsal. Now she just had to get through dinner. Then she'd have twelve glorious hours before the wedding festivities began in the morning.

Finally, the servers returned and placed chicken parmesan in front of her. After everyone had their meal and Josh's father asked the blessing, they were invited to eat. She had a generous fork full of chicken and pasta halfway to her mouth when Chelsea leaned close. Her overwhelming floral perfume tickled Rylee's nose and she resisted the urge to sneeze.

"I heard you and the best man have been spending plenty of time together. How's that going?"

Lord, please give me patience.

Rylee offered up a silent prayer, then swallowed. Unfortunately, her silence invited more unwelcome commentary.

"You looked adorable holding his baby that day while he played cornhole," Chelsea continued, pinning her with a meaningful look. "And the two of you looked like you were made for each other when you walked down the aisle at the rehearsal today."

Oof. Rylee's fork slipped from her hand and clattered on the table. Marinara sauce spattered the white linen.

"Oh, my." Chelsea scootched her chair back in a dramatic attempt to shield her pale blue sundress.

"Sorry," Rylee mumbled, retrieving her fork.

"And let's just acknowledge that he is so handsome. Am I right?" Chelsea grinned. She had lettuce stuck between her teeth. Rylee didn't bother to let her know.

"Sam and I are friends, Chelsea. Since he's here to acquire Hearts Bay Aviation, and I work for Paul and Libby, it makes sense that we'd spend time together."

Despite her best efforts to remain calm, she could feel the blood rushing to her face.

"Then you won't mind if I flirt shamelessly and pull him onto the dance floor tomorrow night." Chelsea waggled her honey-brown eyebrows. "The man looks like he knows how to move."

Oh, my. Rylee shook her head in disbelief. "Even if I did mind, that's never stopped you before."

Chelsea frowned, then playfully swatted Rylee's arm. "Hey, I'm not interested in stepping into your territory, so if you like him, say the word, and I'll back off."

Rylee twirled pasta around her fork, not wanting to have this conversation. She didn't think of Sam as "her territory," but she sure didn't like the idea of ceding that ground either. "You never seem to have a shortage of guys to date."

Chelsea giggled, flipped her hair over one shoulder, then launched into a detailed explanation of her most recent outing with a crab fisherman. Rylee nodded and reacted at what she hoped were the most dramatic parts of Chelsea's story, but she wasn't listening closely.

Her gaze kept wandering against her will to the opposite side of the table. Had Sam heard anything that Chelsea had said? Hopefully not. So embarrassing. He seemed to be fully engaged in his conversation with the man seated to his left.

Chelsea had been obnoxious, but she'd been right about the handsome part. Sam had draped his navy blazer over the back of his chair and rolled the cuffs of his white shirtsleeves back to reveal his tanned forearms. He laughed and clapped the man beside him on the shoulder. A subtle dimple she hadn't noticed before appeared on his right cheek. How had she not seen that?

Last night's tense exchange with her sisters echoed in her head. She should probably apologize for the way she'd stormed out, but the hurt still lingered. Left her feeling unsettled. She was afraid to put herself out there.

Yet she hadn't forgotten how natural it felt to tuck her hand into Sam's as they'd rehearsed the processional at the church earlier today. Or the way he'd smiled and winked when they had taken their places on either side of the altar.

As much as she didn't want to admit it to Chelsea or her sisters or anyone, really, Sam was quite handsome. And thoughtful. Silas was just about the sweetest baby ever. As long as he ate the right food and got plenty of sleep. Thinking about Silas and his contagious belly laugh made her smile.

"Hmm. I guess you saw this already?" Chelsea held up her phone. Rylee glanced at the image on the screen. Her stomach plummeted. It was a picture of her former boyfriend down on one knee, proposing to her cousin.

"Um, no, I hadn't." Rylee forced the words out. "Thanks for the update."

"Oh." Chelsea's smile vanished and her eyes filled with empathy. "Sorry, I thought you knew."

"We don't exactly keep in touch." Rylee pushed her half-finished meal away and wiped her mouth with her napkin.

Chelsea quietly tucked her phone out of sight. "I'm so sorry."

Me too. Rylee grabbed her water glass and filled her mouth with ice cubes. She aggressively chewed on the pellets and plotted her exit. Could she leave before dessert was served? Would that be rude? Because seeing Tucker's photo proposing to her cousin only reinforced her same old fears.

She wasn't ready to give happily-ever-after a second chance. Not even for a guy as kind, thoughtful and genuine as Sam.

The next evening, Sam stood in the hotel ballroom, watching as wedding guests filled the dance floor. Josh and Crystal's wedding couldn't have gone more smoothly. The weather was perfect, the church had been full and the couple's love for each other had filled every heart with a warm glow—even his. Now he really wanted to dance with Rylee.

Instead, he hovered close to the long tables draped in white tablecloths and loaded with food. He'd finished his meal and held a plastic cup of punch in his hand.

"Dude, have you heard even one word I've said?"

Sam gave the guy the side-eye. Drat. Busted. Not only had he not been listening, but he couldn't remember Josh's cousin's name. Dave? Dan?

"I'm sorry." Sam pasted on a polite smile. "What were you saying?"

"We were talking about golf, and I said I'll give you a call the next time I'm in Seattle and we can play your favorite course."

Golf. Right. Sam didn't have the heart to mention he'd rarely golfed before Silas, and now that he was his nephew's guardian, he couldn't envision taking an entire day away from the sweet little fella to swing a club.

"Sure, give me a call." Sam nodded noncommittally but he was already staring across the room where Rylee danced underneath the mirrored ball in the middle of the crowded floor.

With her arms overhead, swaying in time to the music, and her head angled to one side as she smiled at her friends, Rylee looked so free and beautiful that Sam couldn't look away. The other bridesmaids encircled Crystal, who had been alternating between dancing with her friends and her new husband. Josh and Crystal both seemed to be having a fantastic evening.

Sam's chest pinched with envy. If only he could say the same.

The guy turned and followed Sam's line of sight. "Ah. Now I see why you haven't been able to string three words together." He chuckled. "Which one are you after? Chelsea? Or Rylee?"

Sam gritted his teeth. Was he that pathetically obvious?

"Why don't you go over there and ask her to dance?"

Because I'm a coward.

Sam shrugged and glanced down at the plastic cup of punch in his hand. He took a long sip. The sweet fruity drink tasted fine, but didn't help him clear his head.

What if he'd misread the chemistry between him and Rylee? When Josh and Crystal had exchanged rings and recited their vows, it was all Sam could do not to stare at Rylee. She had stood just behind Crystal, blinking back tears and clutching the bride's bouquet. Sure, he was supposed to witness this union, and he had. But he'd also noted that Rylee looked stunning with her hair pinned back at the sides and the rest twisted in long silky ringlets. More than once, he'd imagined running his fingers through those mesmerizing curls.

Stop. He polished off the last of his punch as his adrenaline spiked. If this guy said even one thing about approaching Rylee, Sam would have to find a way to get across the dance floor quickly. Because he was not about to let anybody else dance with her.

"I wonder when they're gonna cut that cake?" Dave tipped his head toward the three-tiered concoction displayed on a small table nearby. Sam had a detailed schedule of the day's events on his phone. So far, he hadn't had to use it. He'd spent the day doing what the wedding coordinator asked him to do, and making sure Josh had everything he needed to enjoy his big day. Dinner was finished, they'd given their toasts, and the requisite dances had been completed. Now the guests were simply celebrating and enjoying themselves. Bass pumped from the speakers and laughter echoed off the walls of the gorgeous venue. It really was a perfect night.

Almost perfect, anyway. The only thing missing was the sensation of Rylee in his arms, swaying to a romantic ballad.

If he didn't ask her to dance soon, he might not get another opportunity. Silas had a babysitter until midnight. The young lady had already texted Sam to let him know that Silas was asleep. He didn't have anything else to worry about other than to help Josh and Crystal get to the airport later.

"Excuse me, please. Great seeing you." Sam clapped the guy on the shoulder, then tossed his cup in the receptacle and made his way across the dance floor. He wasn't the worst dancer in the world, although cutting in on a group of bridesmaids wasn't his typical wedding reception behavior. But before he could even get to Rylee, she turned and made a beeline for the nearest exit.

She needed some air. Crystal motioned for her from the middle of the dance floor to join the rest of the bridal party. Rylee politely shook her head and pointed to the exit. She'd fulfilled her duties as the maid of honor. Gone above and beyond the call of duty, actually. Her feet hurt and her back ached. She was grumpy, to say the least, and all she wanted the new Mr. and Mrs. to do was cut the cake.

Not exactly the festive party mood she'd

hoped for. Guilt niggled her insides as she strode toward the double doors at the back of the reception hall. She scooted past a group of guests lingering near the chocolate fountain.

"Excuse me, please." She smiled and waved to some friends from high school. With her slingbacks in hand, she stepped through the door and out into the unseasonably warm evening air. The sun hovered near the mountains, casting a violet-tinged glow across the lush green hillside. She crossed the freshly mowed lawn. The grass felt cool against her bare feet. Her painfully uncomfortable shoes bumped against her taffeta skirt as she walked.

This was probably not her best move. Mosquitoes would likely feast on her skin. But after standing at the altar and staring into Sam's gorgeous eyes and trying to ignore how handsome he looked in his black tuxedo, she'd been flustered for the rest of the day. Why did he have to look so good? She'd tried and failed several times to avert her eyes, to focus on Josh and Crystal as they'd said their vows and exchanged rings.

Except, after they'd shared their first kiss as husband and wife, a nasty pang of jealousy had sliced right through her. Despite all of her posturing and her claims that she loved her single independent life, seeing one of her friends get married, with the absolutely off-limits Sam Frazier standing just inches away, had given her pause. Made her wonder if she had become a coward. But Sam couldn't be the guy for her. His passion was most definitely not aviation. Now that the wedding was over, he'd have this acquisition wrapped up and be on his way back to Seattle. Other than that flightseeing trip she'd promised him, there wasn't much else keeping him in Hearts Bay.

He certainly wouldn't stay for her.

Not when this whole trip had basically been his exit strategy from the family business. Seattle, his close friends and more people to help with Silas offered far more appeal than this small island community. At least, that's what she'd been telling herself. And, oh, the fleet of nannies he'd probably lined up by now. Besides, his commitment to making sure people had clean water to drink was so admirable. So Sam. There was no way she'd ask him to choose her over making the world a better place. Despite her heart-to-heart with Annie after the Fourth of July party, that elusive courage they'd discussed hadn't materialized.

Okay, so maybe her pride was getting in the way. But why would he ever consider building a life in Hearts Bay? She looked both ways and then crossed the street. Hoping that a few minutes standing at the railing overlooking the water would help her clear her head. Give her the reset she needed to go back to the reception. She stopped on the boardwalk, carefully set her shoes on the ground and leaned on the railing. The metal was cool against her arms and she stared out over the water.

A fishing boat cut across the bay, once again reminding her of her brother, Charlie. He'd always given such great advice. If he were here, what would he tell her to do? Seagulls called to one another as they flew over the harbor. The familiar aroma of saltwater and fish teased her senses. Muffled music from the speakers on the dance floor inside filtered toward her as the doors opened again.

"Mind if I join you?"

Her breath hitched. She turned. Sam stood close by. His crisp white dress shirt offered a sharp contrast to his dark hair.

"Sure." She lifted one shoulder, feigning nonchalance. He couldn't see her pulse thrumming at the base of her throat. Could he?

"I have to admit, I'm following you."

And now he was flirting? Could he be any more irresistible? She swallowed hard. "Is that so?"

"If the MOH can leave the reception, then so can the best man. Am I right?"

"I don't think the place will fall apart without us."

He chuckled. The sound made her heart kick against her ribs. Stop. And hadn't she just talked herself out of falling for him? Apparently, the words hadn't registered. Not in the way that mattered.

Sam's smile faded. His features grew serious. "Everything all right?"

She ducked her head and turned back toward the water, leaning on the railing again. "I just needed some fresh air, that's all."

He nodded, then glanced overhead. "Same. It sure is a gorgeous night."

"Look." She pointed toward the water. "A bald eagle is fishing for its dinner."

Sam leaned on the railing beside her. Together, they watched the majestic bird swoop down and hover over the bay. Its yellow beak, white head and massive wingspan never ceased to amaze her. In one elegant, fluid motion, the eagle captured a salmon in its talons and flew away.

"That was incredible." Sam turned to face her. "I've lived near the Pacific Ocean and Puget Sound for my entire life and I've never seen an eagle catch a fish before."

"We expect our birds of prey to put on a show for our out-of-town guests. It's all part of Hearts Bay's charm."

"Is that so?"

His eyes roamed her face. Even if a dozen eagles descended to snatch salmon from the water, she wouldn't be able to look away. Something kindled in his gaze. Was he leaning closer?

"Are you having a good time? At the reception? Inside?"

Oh, brother. That was the opposite of charming. But she had to at least try to form a coherent sentence. Because standing here staring at him was only going to make things awkward.

He reached over and twined one of her loose curls around his finger. "I'm having a great time now that I'm out here with you."

She gulped a breath. "Really?"

Sam nodded. They were only inches apart. He gently gathered her hair in his hand and brushed it behind her shoulder. The familiar spicy scent of his aftershave enveloped her, teasing her senses. When he rested his palm on the curve of her waist, she forgot all about her maid of honor responsibilities and how much she'd been looking forward to a slice of that wedding cake. Did anyone inside even notice they were gone?

There was still time to correct the course. Still time for her to pick up her shoes and walk away. But she couldn't think of one single reason why she should go. She let her palm slide up his arm, then pressed up on her toes and brushed her lips against his. Slow and sweet. His mouth was warm and he tasted like fruit punch. Her only regret? That they'd waited so long to kiss.

Except, he wasn't kissing her back.

Oh, no. Oh, no, no, no. Rylee pushed away. Shame heated her skin. "I'm so sorry. I don't know what I was thinking. I should have never…"

She leaned down, scooped up her shoes and quickly hurried back to the reception. She'd stick around long enough to see Crystal and Josh cut the cake, but she most definitely would not be available for the bouquet toss. Crystal needed her help to change and then she'd have to stay until the end when Josh and Crystal drove away. Tears threatened to fall. Breaking into a jog, she tamped down a sob. She could do this. She could be strong. She'd finish out the night because she'd given her word. She'd fall apart later when she was alone.

"Rylee, wait."

Her skirt trailed behind her like a cape as she ran toward the back doors of the hotel and the reception venue. What had he done? This was all his fault. He hadn't meant to *not* kiss her. She'd looked up at him, her thick lashes fluttering against her flawless skin and something like adoration swimming in her eyes, and he'd lost all sense of reason.

One minute, they'd been harmlessly flirting and the next, he'd touched her hair. The strands were silky and softer than he'd imagined. And he was certain that he'd been the first to lean closer. When he'd placed his hand on her waist, what else was she supposed to think?

No, he couldn't blame her for closing the distance and kissing him. He'd be lying if he said he hadn't savored the sensation of her lips against his. Achingly sweet. Pliant. And she'd smelled incredible. Her hand clasped against his arm had made him want to pull her into an embrace and deepen the kiss.

But then he'd panicked. Started overthinking the whole scenario. How would he manage Silas and a romantic relationship? His family was about to acquire her employer. And she lived here. Hearts Bay was lovely but it felt about a gazillion miles away from Seattle. As soon as he tied up all the loose ends associated with the acquisition's due diligence period, he'd be on his way home.

But then what? His stomach twisted into a knot. What if he came back? Someone from Frazier Aviation had to relocate. Why couldn't he be that guy? Maybe if he volunteered for the role, his father wouldn't be so disappointed with him.

Snippets of his last conversation with the project manager in Nicaragua flitted through his head. He couldn't let his people down. He'd already committed to ambitious fundraising goals and providing new wells in three villages. Now was not the time to turn his life upside down. Not when he'd lost his brother and Erin less than a month ago. Silas had already been robbed of so much. Sam couldn't bring himself to completely uproot the baby from their entire support network.

"Rylee, please, can we talk about this?"

A horn blared and he jumped out of the way. A diesel-engine truck rumbled by and the driver gestured in anger through the window. Whoa. That was close. The vehicle had nearly barreled across his toes. His heart hammered in his chest. Pausing, he glanced both ways. When the street was clear, he cut long strides across the pavement.

Rylee was almost back to the reception. He jogged after her and caught up before she slipped inside.

"Please. Wait. I'm so sorry," he said, bracing one hand against the door.

She gripped the door handle and turned toward him. Her cheeks were flushed. Her thorny look gutted him. "You don't have to be sorry. I was completely out of line. That should not have happened."

"Well, I don't know if I'd go that far." He palmed the back of his neck. It had been a pretty great kiss. Until he'd wrecked everything. "It's just…complicated."

She arched one brow. "Is it? Seems you've made your feelings quite clear to me."

"Have I?"

Her breath rushed out with a groan. "Are you trying to make this worse?"

"No, of course not." Sam held up both palms, desperate to defuse her anger. "I'm trying to apologize."

"I already told you, this was my mistake. I shouldn't have kissed you." Her mouth set at an unforgiving angle, she tugged the door open. "We need to go inside and pretend this never happened. Josh and Crystal deserve our full attention."

He opened his mouth to protest but then pinched his lips tight. "Right. Of course."

Shoving his hands in his pockets, he stepped back and gave her space. There was no point in arguing with her. She'd made up her mind. Besides, what could he say? He hadn't meant to hurt her. And now she wanted nothing to do with him.

Chapter Ten

Twenty-four miserable hours later, Rylee stood outside Heath and Lexi's house, desperate for a shoulder to cry on. Sharp evening sunlight cut across the lawn, and she squinted, looking around for signs of her sister.

"Come on, please be home." She rang the doorbell again, then peered through the rectangular window beside the door. Heath's truck sat parked in the driveway. Scout's bark punctuated the air. Surely they'd answer soon. If not, she'd circle around the house and check the backyard.

Because she refused to spend a second night in a row sobbing into her pillow.

She rang the bell again and silently prayed for help. Sure, she could move on to one of her other sisters, but Lexi seemed the most receptive to hearing about her heartache.

Muffled footsteps approached, the dead bolt turned and the door swung open. Lexi stood there, looking positively adorable in a pair of white jeans and a green sleeveless top with a crocheted inset around the neckline. Her glossy dark hair had been twisted into two braids. Dangly beaded earrings sparkled as she tilted her head to one side and offered a sweet smile.

"Hey, Rylee." Even after all these months in Hearts Bay, Lexi still hadn't lost her Southern accent. "What brings you by?"

Rylee held out the white cardboard bakery box. "I have cupcakes and I'm not afraid to grovel."

Chuckling, Lexi stepped back and waved her in. "You don't need to grovel and cupcakes are always welcome."

Rylee stepped inside and closed the door. A discarded princess costume, an array of plastic blocks and one of Scout's stuffed dog toys were strewn about the floor. Folded laundry sat stacked neatly on the back of Lexi's green-velvet sofa.

"If I'd known you were coming by, I would have picked up a little bit," Lexi said. "Heath and Molly Jo are in the backyard. I convinced him to put up a play structure so we've been outside as much as possible."

Rylee stepped out of her canvas slip-on shoes

and left them under a bench in the entryway. "Molly Jo must be having a ball."

"She's gone down the slide about fifty times today. I don't know if we'll ever get her inside for her bath." Lexi cleared a stack of folded baby blankets from the end of the sofa. "Have a seat. Would you like some coffee or tea to go with your cupcake?"

"I'd love to drown my sorrows in some decaf coffee, if you have any." Rylee slid the box of cupcakes onto the wooden coffee table and flopped back against the sofa's tufted cushions. "I know I have no right to ask for your help after the way I stormed out of here last week, but I could really use some advice."

"You didn't storm out of here. We ganged up on you, and I'm sorry about that." Lexi leaned closer and examined Rylee's hands. "Your manicure still looks great, by the way."

Rylee splayed her fingers in front of her sister. She couldn't help but laugh. "You deserve all the credit. I've tried hard not to mess them up. Back to work tomorrow, though, so no promises."

Lexi gently patted her arm. "I'll be right back with your coffee and some plates and napkins. If Molly Jo comes inside, throw one of those blankets over the cupcake box. The girl does not need any more sugar this close to bedtime."

Rylee grimaced. "Argh, I'm so sorry. I shouldn't have come by and interrupted your evening routine."

"Nonsense," Lexi called over her shoulder as she moved into the kitchen. "You absolutely can interrupt my evening anytime."

Rylee surveyed Lexi and Heath's family room and soaked in the comfort of her sister's inviting home. Cupboard doors opened and closed. Plates clinked together, then the coffeemaker gurgled to life. Through the open living room window, Molly Jo's squeals coupled with Heath's deep voice filtered in.

Lexi had added a new family photo to her collection displayed on the bookshelf nearby. Heath stood at the edge of the water, Hearts Bay's iconic rocky outcropping in the background. Lexi leaned close, her arm looped around his waist. Scout sat at Lexi's feet, his copper curls sprung up at jaunty angles. The photo had captured his pink tongue lolling from one side of his open mouth. Molly Jo stood beside Heath, her little arm anchored around his leg. Their hair was messy and wind-blown but they all had the biggest smiles on their faces.

Rylee's heart pinched. She looked away and massaged the ache in her chest with her fingertips. Is this what she wanted? A loving husband, kids posed for frameable photos, and summer evenings in the backyard? If she was honest, the answer was yes. All of the above. But twice she'd put herself out there and twice she'd been rejected. She could fly an airplane through a storm, and land on a runway carved between mountains and the ocean, but when it came to love, she just couldn't get past the fear.

"Here we are." Lexi returned carrying a tray with two small plates, napkins, utensils and a carton of creamer. She eased the tray onto the coffee table. "Let me get your coffee."

Rylee lifted the lid on the box of cupcakes. She'd picked a dozen from the leftovers at Josh and Crystal's reception.

Lexi set the steaming mug of coffee on a coaster. "That's going to need a minute to cool off. Help yourself to creamer and there are a few sugar packets here somewhere."

"Thanks so much." Rylee gestured toward the box. "These are from last night."

Lexi eyed the frosted cupcakes. "Oh, my. Are those red velvet?"

"With cream cheese frosting."

"Yes, please." Lexi plucked the red velvet cupcake from the box, set it on a plate and quickly peeled back the paper. "I haven't had one of these in ages. They are my absolute favorite."

"Enjoy." Rylee plated a chocolate cupcake

with vanilla frosting, set it on the coffee table, then she stirred cream and sugar into her coffee.

Lexi licked a dollop of frosting from her fingertip. "All right. Lay it on me. What happened?"

Rylee hesitated. "Last night at the reception I went outside to cool off. I wanted to get some fresh air and take a break from the dancing."

"Uh-huh. Go on," Lexi said around a mouthful of cupcake.

"Sam decided to join me. We were talking, and flirting, and I thought we were having a moment. Before you know it, I'm thinking about how great he smells and I can't stop staring at his lips, and then I kissed him."

Lexi gasped. She put down her half-finished cupcake and clapped her hands "Rylee, way to go! I'm so proud of you."

"You're not going to be impressed when I tell you what happened next."

"Oh, no."

"He wasn't that into it." The words left her mouth in a rush. She covered her face with her hands. Even now, admitting the truth out loud to her sweet sister, she was still so embarrassed.

Ashamed.

"Oh, sweetie." Lexi rubbed her back. "What did he say?"

"He didn't have to say anything." Rylee dropped her hands to her lap. "His body language said it all. He didn't kiss me back."

"Maybe he's nervous about starting a relationship when he's about to leave the island," Lexi said.

"That's the proverbial mountain between us."

Lexi sighed. "I'm so sorry that this has happened. It's especially painful to be rejected this way."

"Again. Rejected *again*." Rylee shook her head, forming her hands into fists. "Why did this have to happen? First Tucker and now Sam. What am I supposed to do?"

"I hate that I don't have any easy answers," Lexi said quietly. "Did you try talking to him?"

"That didn't go so well." Rylee reached for her coffee. "He followed me back to the reception, but I was too angry to really hear what he had to say."

"That's certainly understandable."

"We still have to see each other because he's here for three more days." Lexi stared into her steaming mug. "That's going to be super awkward."

"I'm going to pray that any good that can come from this will unfold quickly. The story is not over yet. He hasn't left the island. Of course your feelings are hurt, but you're both adults, so you can work through this if the two of you are meant to be."

"I want to believe that. I mean, I do believe that the Lord is working everything for our good. But this just seems so unfair. Why did Sam and Silas come into my life if they're both just going to be yanked away by the end of the week?" Rylee blinked back tears. "I don't understand."

Unshed tears shimmered in Lexi's golden-brown eyes. "I know you're hurting, but I am certain that this will get better. We're your family and we love you and you're going to get through this."

"Thank you," Rylee whispered. Another wave of emotion crested inside as she rested her head on Lexi's shoulder and let the tears fall. So much for vowing that she wouldn't cry about Sam today. At least she wasn't crying alone.

Lexi was right. She had to trust that the Lord had not forgotten her. That He understood the longings of her heart, even though she'd been crushed in the past. A tiny part of her wished that she had never kissed Sam Frazier, because now she knew what she was missing.

Three days. Seventy-two hours. As a numbers guy, Sam had always found comfort in predictable metrics. Deadlines provided clear expectations and there was nothing obscure about the fact that he had an exit strategy. By Wednesday, he'd be off this island.

Too bad the notion of saying goodbye to Rylee so soon planted a hollow ache in his gut.

After their kiss-gone-wrong on Saturday evening, he'd spent most of yesterday trying and failing to come up with a plan to make things right. He'd gone to church, seen Rylee there and had wanted to talk to her, to explain, but with Silas in tow, he'd been surrounded by people cooing over the happy baby after the service. Rylee had left before he could break free.

"Buh, buh, buh," Silas babbled. "Buh!"

"All right, all right, I'm listening." Sam glanced down at the blanket he'd spread on the floor of their suite for Silas to enjoy some tummy time. "You clever boy."

Silas had pushed up on his hands and knees. Drooling, he rocked back and forth on all fours. Each syllable he spoke got progressively louder.

"Whoa, this is new." Sam lunged for his phone where he'd left it on the desk, then sank to the floor beside the blanket. "Show me your best moves, pal."

Grinning, Silas rocked back and forth. "Buh, buh, buh."

"Nicely done." Sam opened his camera and filmed a quick video. Silas added a few ear-curdling screeches, then made up for it with another slobbery grin and an infectious giggle.

Chuckling, Sam zoomed in and recorded for a few more seconds. He didn't want to miss any of Silas's milestones. Mom had already sent him a text this morning, asking for a new picture. Erin's parents had thanked him profusely after he'd sent them three photos last week. A glimpse of a white bump in Silas's red gums distracted him. He stopped the video and put his phone down.

"Dude, is that a tooth? Are you seriously going to learn to crawl and get teeth all at the same time? That does not sound fun."

Silas collapsed on his tummy and started to cry.

"No worries, my man. You'll have this figured out in no time."

He mentally made a note to research later what teething babies needed. Based on the few things his friends who had kids had mentioned, the phase didn't sound especially fun.

Silas lifted his head. Fat tears tracked down his flushed cheeks.

"Aww, come here." Sam gently scooped Silas into his arms and checked the time on his phone. He had a video call with his parents in a couple of minutes. If Silas took a nap, they'd have a peaceful mostly stress-free call.

Not that Dad wouldn't pelt him with a dozen questions. Sam was ready, though. He had done his due diligence. Except for his flight with Rylee. Libby had helped him reschedule a one-hour trip tomorrow. He hadn't looked at the weather forecast yet. Maybe they'd have to cancel. Again.

After changing Silas's diaper, Sam tucked him in his crib in the suite's extra bedroom. He gave him a pacifier and his favorite stuffed frog. Silas's expression crumpled. His pitiful cries made Sam pause beside the crib. He really hated upsetting him, but there was no way his father would tolerate a screaming baby in the middle of a conference call.

"I've got to get some work done. When you wake up, we'll have lunch and go for a stroll outside." Sam left the room and closed the door quietly. He returned to the desk and made sure his portable baby monitor beside the TV was turned on. Then he opened his computer and waited for his father to call.

Silas kept crying. Sam's scalp prickled. He adjusted the volume on the monitor. Maybe he shouldn't have given the babysitter the day off. An extra set of hands would've been prudent during this call. But after Silas had spent Friday evening and all of Saturday with babysitters, Sam had felt guilty leaving him again.

Since Rylee wasn't real interested in speaking with him, he didn't have much on his calendar today. He'd hoped they might be able to talk for a few minutes this afternoon, but Libby had given him a peek at today's flight schedule and Rylee was booked solid. Probably for the best. She'd already accused him of making things worse. How many different ways could he apologize without her getting more upset?

An alert pinged on his phone. He retrieved the device from where he'd tossed it on the bed. A message from Rylee appeared on the screen. His heart sputtered.

Double-checking your availability for tomorrow. I need to file my flight plan. We're scheduled to depart from Hearts Bay airport at 10 a.m. Does that still work for you?

Sam blew out a breath. There was so much he wanted to say. He scrubbed his hand across his face and reread the message. Before the acquisition was complete, someone from Frazier needed to have flown at least once with a local pilot. Sure, he could have asked Rylee to swap out with Carson, but that felt incredibly petty.

The last thing he wanted to do was to hurt her more than he already had.

Thanks for checking in. Ten sounds great. Looking forward to it.

He sent the message before he had time to overthink it. Setting his phone aside, he logged into the video call from his laptop. A moment later, his father's and mother's faces appeared on the screen.

"Hello, son." Dad's weathered features formed a weary smile. "How are you?"

"I'm well, Dad. Hi, Mom. How are you?"

His mother leaned in toward the camera. At least she'd combed her hair and put on something other than her bathrobe. That was progress. The last time they'd spoken, Dad had mentioned his mother hadn't been taking care of herself.

"I'm all right, sweetie. Getting a little less sad each day." Her smile faltered. "How are you? How's that adorable grandson of ours? You haven't sent me a picture in a while."

Sam winced. "Sorry about that. Silas is doing great. I just took a video of him. He's figured out how to push up from his tummy onto all fours. I'll send it to you as soon as we're finished chatting."

"Sounds good. I'll be waiting." She stood, bracing her hand on his father's chair for support. How long had her shoulders been hunched forward like that? Wow, she looked older than the last time he'd seen her. How was that possible? He hadn't been gone for long. Grief had certainly taken the wind out of her sails.

"Talk to you soon, Mom."

"I hope you two have a productive conversation. See you soon." She swiveled carefully and blew a kiss toward the camera. "Can't wait until you and Silas are home."

Aww, she'd really missed them. Sam waved. "Thanks, Mom. Love you."

"Love you too." She gave his father a gentle pat on the shoulder, then walked slowly toward the door of his father's home office. She went out and closed the door behind her.

His father wasted no time getting straight to the point. Sam had planned to ask how he thought Mom was coping. Evidently, nothing personal was on the agenda.

"The board and I are quite pleased with all the progress you've made so far." Dad slipped his reading glasses on and scanned the documents he held in his hands. "The due diligence period is drawing to a close. What's your recommendation?"

"I have no concerns, Dad. Libby emailed me

additional documents on Friday. Profit and loss statements, a copy of their business license, copies of land use and building permits. Minutes from the last town council meeting when they discussed adding an addition to the airport and improving the runway. They have some reasonable and customary debt. Nothing alarming. Paul and Libby have done a fantastic job. You really would—"

"When will you evaluate their aircraft and review maintenance logs?" Dad interrupted. "Is the fleet aging? How many years of experience does their mechanic have?"

"Hold on." Sam held up a hand. "I didn't get that far yet."

Dad frowned. "You haven't reviewed their maintenance logs or spoken with their mechanic? Why not? That's a crucial aspect of the merger. We need to know if we have to hire additional mechanics and technicians. We'll be looking at a significant increase in payroll, which means cutting back their current staff. Those fellas aren't cheap, you know."

Sam bit his lip to keep from saying something snide. In all the mountains of paperwork and instructions from Frazier's interim COO, he'd never once seen anything about maintenance logs or evaluating the fleet. Wasn't that

Paul and Libby's responsibility to disclose any issues?

He grabbed his phone and opened a note app. "Let's run through those questions one more time, please."

Dad barreled through his expectations again.

Sam's fingers flew over his keyboard as he typed the info into his phone. When he finished, he met his father's doubtful gaze. "Don't worry. I've got this."

He didn't have it. Not at all. Sure, he'd had one conversation with Rylee about her coworkers and the pilot cutting his hours back, but that didn't indicate a staffing issue. Did it? Libby had been completely transparent when he'd shadowed her for a few hours. Was she supposed to hand over purchase orders or invoices for parts? If she had, he wouldn't have known how to analyze the data. But he wasn't about to admit that now. Dad and the rest of the company's leadership team were counting on him to see this through.

He set his phone aside and met his father's piercing stare on screen. "Everyone at Hearts Bay Aviation has been extremely easy to work with. I'm not aware of any personnel issues. I'm scheduled for a flight tomorrow, a local tour of the area. The pilot taking me up is excellent, and I'm confident she'll be able to answer any questions."

If she'll speak to me.

Another key detail he'd refrain from sharing right now. Dad didn't need to know that he'd muddled his personal and professional lives.

An awkward silence prevailed. Sam squirmed in his chair. "Dad, are you okay?"

His father's bushy eyebrows scrunched together. "About as well as can be expected, Sam. Thank you for asking."

"You're welcome." Sam snuck a glance at the monitor. Thankfully, Silas had stopped crying. He was huddled in one corner of his crib, pacifier in his mouth and the stuffed animal tucked under his chin. The bands of tension in Sam's chest loosened.

Dad cleared his throat. "Did Josh get married?"

"He did. They're off on their honeymoon in Mexico."

"Good."

"Really good." Sam forced a smile that he hoped was genuine. "They're going to be very happy together."

"All right. Well, nothing further on our end. Let me know when you get those issues addressed. The board of directors would appreciate a spreadsheet detailing all pertinent documentation."

Oh, boy. Sam stifled a groan. "A spreadsheet. Right. I'll take care of it."

"I know you will."

They exchanged goodbyes and Sam clicked the button to end the call, sighing and leaning back in his desk chair. How had he overlooked those details? So much for having this thing all wrapped up. Even though his last conversation with Rylee had ended poorly, he'd have to ask more questions during their flight tomorrow. And request more information from Paul and Libby. As much as he wanted to be finished with his part of the acquisition, he couldn't leave the island knowing he hadn't fulfilled his commitment to his family and their business.

Chapter Eleven

Following that pod of orcas had seemed like a brilliant idea. Until it wasn't.

From inside the Super Cub's cockpit, Rylee gripped the control stick and scanned the horizon through the small plane's windshield. The ominous cloud bank looming ahead made her palms clammy. She'd checked and double-checked the forecast. Texted another pilot who'd made a quick flight to the north side of the island early this morning. He'd reported excellent visibility and winds at seven knots.

Thankfully, Sam was seated behind her and couldn't see the anxious thoughts undoubtedly written all over her face.

She'd flown Sam west from Hearts Bay airport, giving him the full aerial flightseeing tour that she'd offer any of their paying customers. After she'd circled over the village where her grandmother lived, she'd planned to head home. Except she'd spotted the killer whales feeding off the coast. Instead of cutting directly across the island, she'd banked her trusty aircraft to the right and soared over the Gulf of Alaska. Watching the sleek animals swimming through the waters, then diving deep only to surface again was simply breathtaking.

Sam had probably witnessed similar pods feeding in Puget Sound, but she still couldn't resist granting him a glimpse from the air. If he had been a customer, she most definitely would've rerouted to give them the same opportunity. This flightseeing tour not only marked the end of his visit but his final activity with Hearts Bay Aviation. Given how things had gone between them on Saturday night, she desperately wanted to be the consummate professional today. Her need to impress him had forced her into a tenuous situation, though.

"Is everything okay?" Sam's voice crackled through her headset. "You haven't said a word since we flew over those whales."

So, he had noticed. To fill the silence, she'd chattered almost nonstop since takeoff over an hour ago. "I'm a bit concerned about the weather."

"Can you fly through those clouds? They look pretty dark."

She bit her lip and sat up straighter, willing their surroundings to improve. Her hand ached from gripping the control stick, and the stress of navigating through a storm had her muscles all bunched together as she peered through the windshield searching for an opening in the clouds.

"I have to make an emergency landing." Icy terror crawled up the back of her throat.

"Land where?"

"I'm sorry, Sam. I know it's not ideal, but I can't see through this fog. Visibility has dropped. There are mountains between here and home. I fly using VFR, which means visual flight rules. And if I…"

She trailed off, unable to finish spelling out the worst-case scenario. Her Super Cub was lightweight and reliable. Perfect for short runways and challenging takeoffs. But experience had taught her not to rely too much on her aircraft. Or to pretend she had superhuman capabilities to see around storms. If she made a poor choice and kept flying, the results could be disastrous.

"How will we get back?" Sam asked.

"As soon as the weather improves, we'll be back in the air and on our way."

"And if the weather doesn't improve?"

She swallowed hard. "Then we wait out the

storm and fly when it's safe. I left a flight plan
with Carson. I'll try to hail him on the radio
and give him an update. If we don't come back
on time, he'll activate search and rescue."

His heavy sigh made her wince.

"You say that so casually. Like you're going
for a trip to the grocery store."

"There's nothing casual about what I'm proposing. For the sake of transparency, I'm explaining that this is how aviation in Alaska
works. We learn to be prepared for anything.
I have to do my job, and that means getting us
safely on the ground."

She adjusted her rudder pedals, then guided
the stick forward. The plane began a slow de-
scent.

"Where will you land?"

"There's a clearing not far from here."

"How do you know? Have you landed there
before?"

"No, but I fly over twice a week. The guy
raised cattle and kept horses. His wife used
to have chickens and a goat. Can you believe
that? He's not keeping cattle there now, as far
as I know. At least, not the last time I checked.
I've been—"

"Rylee, you're babbling," Sam interrupted.
"Do you need to call ahead or something?"

She barked out a laugh. "No time for that.

Besides, he doesn't have a phone. Relies on the radio mostly and…never mind."

"Fill me in later."

"Right." She glanced out the window to the right and left, checking for any obstructions in the grassy field below. Her heart hammered in her chest. She could do this. She'd completed emergency landings due to weather and lack of fuel before, although never on this part of the island.

"So this guy with the cattle, he's used to planes randomly landing in his field?"

"No, but an unscheduled landing in the field is better than a plane coming apart over his house."

"That is *not* what I need to hear right now."

"I know, I know. You don't appreciate my sense of humor, and I hate that we're in this situation, and I'm so very sorry. Let's focus on landing this plane safely."

"*You* can focus on landing this plane. I'm no help." His voice grew louder. "I'm not a pilot, remember?"

Panic welled inside. She battled it back. "Deep breaths, Sam. It's best to remain calm."

Please, please don't let me miscalculate our location.

She silently flung up the prayer, then checked the fuel gauge and her oil pressure. Carson had modified this plane with an extra-large fuel tank. Even though the needle hovered closer to empty than she'd prefer, he'd taught her that she could count on having an additional eight gallons beyond what the gauge indicated.

Through the wispy clouds encircling the plane, she spotted the red metal roof in the distance. "That's the Knutsen property. I recognize the outbuildings. We're almost there."

"Good."

Sam's one-word response didn't exactly inspire confidence, but she couldn't blame him for doubting her. Just when she solved one problem, another cropped up. She was coming in too fast. Rain blew across her windshield in sheets. Her mouth went dry. She had enough fuel for a go-around, but what if the fog closed in on her second approach and she couldn't see to land?

"You're coming in hot, aren't you?"

"A little bit." She forced the words through her clenched teeth and pulled back on the stick, determined to slow their approach.

"Hold on!" The grassy field rushed up to meet them and all three of her wheels hit the ground hard. They weren't slowing down quickly enough. She stomped on the brake. The pungent scent of burning rubber stung her nostrils. Thankfully, there weren't any animals grazing, but the massive trees at the end of the property were coming up fast.

"Rylee, Rylee, Rylee!" Sam yelled her name over and over, quadrupling her terror. She screamed, squeezed her eyes shut and flung her hands in the air to protect her face.

Sam wiggled his toes inside his sneakers. Then opened and closed his fists. No issues. He scanned the interior of the plane. Rain pummeled the outside, but they were dry and everything appeared to be intact. He peeked through the windshield. Dark green tree branches formed a canopy over the nose of the plane, so close, the propeller almost touched tree bark.

He unbuckled his seat belt and scooted forward. Reaching out, he gently clasped Rylee's shoulder. The canvas material on her jacket felt cool against his warm palm. "Are you okay?"

She twisted to face him. Her ashen expression made his chest ache. She was scared. "I—I'm fine. A little rattled, but nothing's broken. You?"

He pulled away, glanced down and gave himself another quick once-over. "I'm okay. Totally panicked there for a second, but I'm thrilled that you got us on the ground. Thank you."

"You're welcome." She paused, as if she wanted to say more.

He was not proud of the way he'd flipped out. But wouldn't anyone in his position be a bit concerned? Just because he belonged to a family that loved aviation didn't mean he had the same zest for backcountry flying adventures.

"The plane's hopefully all in one piece." She leaned over, her features pinched with exertion. "Let me find my phone and check for a signal."

"Do we need to get out? Smells like something is burning."

"Friction from the brakes riding against the wheels. If any part of the aircraft had caught fire, we'd know by now." Rylee held up her phone. "No signal for me. How about you?"

He stood and retrieved his backpack from the cargo hold behind his seat. How was she so calm about all this? Man, he'd love to borrow some of that energy. Because right now adrenaline surged through his veins and his legs itched to run. He wiped his hands on his jeans, then fished out his phone.

The screen was dark. He jabbed at the power button. Nothing happened. He wanted to howl in frustration. How had that happened? "My phone's dead."

"We'll get by. I'll try to hail someone on the radio." She produced a handheld walkie-talkie from her bag. "As soon as this fog lifts, I'll need you to get out and help me turn the plane around."

He slumped in his seat and stared at her. "Why?"

"So we can taxi and take off again." Irritation flashed in her eyes. "You do want to get back to Hearts Bay today, right?"

"You don't need to check the plane for damage or anything?" That had been quite the hairy landing. Not to mention this field looked nothing like a suitable runway.

She hesitated, the walkie-talkie halfway to her mouth. "I'll run through my normal pre-flight checklist. If everything is satisfactory, we can take off as soon as the skies are clear."

He opened his mouth to protest. The pointed look she gave him made him think twice. Instead, he pressed his lips closed and tried to turn his phone on again.

Still nothing. Unbelievable. He'd charged the thing overnight. How did he not have any power at all? He half listened as Rylee tried to contact someone on the radio. Only static came through the walkie-talkie speaker. His thoughts turned to Silas. What would the babysitter do if Sam didn't show up at the resort this afternoon as he'd promised? Would she call her parents for help?

Stop. It.

Those questions only jump-started a fresh cycle of fear. He couldn't allow himself to tumble down the rabbit hole of what-ifs. Not when they were still sitting here, riding out a storm and unable to find help.

Rylee tried two more times before dropping the walkie-talkie in her lap. She released a protracted sigh, then tugged a bright yellow rain jacket from the depths of her bag. "All right. No response yet. The sky is getting a smidge brighter, though."

Sam peeked out his tiny window. "It's still raining hard."

A muscle in her jaw twitched. "In about thirty minutes, let's plan on getting out and maneuvering the plane into position. I have an emergency poncho if you didn't pack a rain jacket."

"Um, no. I didn't pack one."

Was he supposed to have emergency provisions in his bag? She'd explained the preflight safety briefing when they'd been on the ground in Hearts Bay. To be honest, he hadn't paid much attention because Carson and Libby were standing nearby, having a conversation about a pilot not showing up for work. Sam had been distracted, wondering if he should ask Rylee to postpone the flight so he could follow up with his unanswered questions. Dad would want that spreadsheet soon, and it still sat unfinished on his laptop back at the resort.

"Sam?"

Rylee's voice brought him back to reality.

"Hmm?"

"Did you hear what I said?"

He nodded. "Thirty minutes. Maneuver the plane. You have a poncho for me."

"Right." She pushed her arms through the rain jacket and shrugged it on, forced to hunch over in the snug cockpit.

"How about if I walk over to that house or one of the outbuildings? I can check and see if anyone's here."

She scraped her palm across her face. "I don't know Mr. Knutsen well, but most people on the island, if you land in their field, they'll be out to ask what you're up to in a couple of minutes."

"So that's a no then."

"I'm trying to save you the trouble. It doesn't seem like anybody's home."

Sighing, he shoved his fingers through his hair. "All right."

Rain pattered on the roof. Rylee stood near the door, hunched over, the yellow hood covering her dark hair. Her narrow-eyed scrutiny made him squirm.

"Sam, do you trust me?"

"What?" He didn't bother to mask his frustration. "Yes, of course. Why?"

"For a guy who's never flown anything, you have a lot of strong opinions about how I'm handling this. If you've got a better idea, believe me, I am open to suggestions."

"To be honest, I'm concerned about you trying to fly in these conditions. But if you can't get anyone to respond on the radio, no one's looking for us, and you feel you can safely get this plane back in the air, then I say, let's go for it."

Again he felt skewered by her doubtful gaze. "Really?"

No.

"Yes. Really."

"Okay, good. I'm going to go out and walk the field. I'll check for any muddy patches, holes, divots or obstructions that might pose a problem."

"What can I do to help?"

She hit him with one last fierce look. "You can pray."

She didn't blame him for being skeptical.

But couldn't he at least pretend that he had faith in her? For a guy who'd spent a ton of time outdoors and had climbed a few mountains,

Sam sure was getting worked up about being stranded in a storm.

Rylee traipsed across the field, kicking at a stone in her path. If he had the solution to their problem, why didn't he just say so? Instead, he sat there fiddling with his dead phone and over-thinking every possible outcome. Maybe she was being a bit too hard on the guy. After all, she'd screamed and thrown her hands over her face. That looked and sounded a lot like panic.

At the last minute, Carson had offered to take this flight. She should've let him. Even though she hadn't told anyone at work about kissing Sam at the wedding reception, she suspected that Libby knew something was up. News like that spread quickly around town. If Carson had heard, he was too kind to give her a hard time about it.

She stopped and glanced up at the gray sky, squinting into the rain. A light breeze wrapped its chilly fingers around her. Shivering, she resumed her examination of Mr. Knutsen's field. This was not a great situation, but it could have been so much worse. The plane was completely unscathed from her emergency landing. She'd done exactly as she had been trained to do. Now she just needed this wind to change direction and the clouds to lift, and they'd be good to go. She scanned the ground for anything that might impede taxiing to takeoff speed. The ground squished under her boots. She noted the soft spot, as well as a patch of mud off to the right. Both were completely avoidable.

Turning around, she strode back to the plane, counting out her steps. Less than a hundred yards was really all she needed, so this could work. She opened the door. Sam was exactly where she'd left him.

"The field looks fine. Will you please come out here and help me? It's not difficult. Super Cubs are incredibly lightweight." She formed her lips into what she hoped was an optimistic smile and infused her voice with confidence. "I expect the weather to improve shortly, and we can get out of here."

Sam nodded. "Let's do it."

"That emergency poncho is in the cargo hold where you had your backpack."

"Thanks. I'll be right there."

She circled the hardworking red-and-white-striped aircraft slowly, mentally reviewing her preflight checklist. All three wheels were still properly inflated. Brakes and pads were functional. There wasn't any evidence of a hydraulic fluid leak or damage to the plane's strut attachments.

Ducking under the belly of the plane, she moved toward the front. Even though her propeller had come dangerously close to the trees lining the edge of the field, once she studied it, she wasn't concerned. It looked great.

Sam hopped out of the plane and landed nimbly on the ground. He quickly slipped the blue poncho over his head and tugged the hood in place. "All right. I'm ready."

"We'll stand on either side of the plane and gently push the wings, guiding the plane backward. It takes some effort, but if we can work together, we can get it turned around. Any questions?"

Sam shook his head and took his place beside the wing. A few minutes later, they had the aircraft maneuvered into position and facing down the field. Rylee whooped and punched the air with her fist. When she met Sam at the cockpit door, she held up her palm.

He gave her a high five, then looked off in the distance. The lines around his mouth drew taut and his masculine brows scrunched together. "I know you're tired of me asking questions, but are you sure this field is long enough?"

Deflated, she bit back a snide comment. He still didn't think this was going to work.

She pointed toward the American flag mounted on a pole near the house. "It's not ideal, but we have the best possible aircraft to make it happen. The Super Cub is known for its stellar ability to perform on short runways. And the wind just changed direction. Visibility has improved. We'll be airborne in a few minutes."

They climbed back inside the plane. Shoving aside her frustration, she forced herself to focus on the task at hand. She primed the engine, put her headset on and stared straight ahead. "Buckle up, please."

Without another word, Sam clicked his seat belt together.

She drew a deep, calming breath, fastened her seat belt and ran through the final tasks on her preflight checklist. The engine started without any hiccups.

Thank you, Lord.

Slowly, she taxied down the field. The wheels sank into a divot and she hesitated. Had too much rain saturated the ground? Her plane shimmied sideways. Uncertainty speared her. Aborting the takeoff wasn't something she'd practiced in ages. Instead, she corrected and they continued down the field.

"It's fine. This is fine," she whispered.

Sam didn't respond.

She scanned the ground up ahead and then the horizon for any hindrances. Seeing none, she advanced the throttle and eased the stick forward. The aircraft picked up speed. Overhead, a beam of sunlight broke through the clouds. When the plane lifted off the ground, she pushed out a relieved breath.

"You've got it, Rylee," Sam said. Through her headset, she thought she heard a smile edging his voice.

Then a terrifying jolt flipped them off course. A sickening sensation swamped her. Instead of climbing higher and soaring toward the patch of blue in the sky overhead, they cartwheeled across the field. Disoriented, the world outside the aircraft spun by in a blur. Her head struck something hard. Pain seared behind her eyes and her world went black.

"Rylee? Can you hear me?"

Sam looked around slowly, trying to assess the damage. The engine had sputtered and died as they'd careened nose-over-tail. An eerie silence filled the air. His fingers trembled as he fumbled with the metal clasp on his seat belt. They were upside down in the field, that much he knew for sure. And he had to get out of this stupid plane.

"Rylee?"

Still no response. Dread slithered in. What if she'd—

He couldn't even finish the thought. Sliding free of the canvas straps that held him in his seat, he inched forward. The plane shuddered, its wings rocking side to side. He hesitated. Should he stay put? But what good would that do?

A muffled groan filtered toward him from the pilot's seat.

"Rylee, come on. Wake up, please. I need you." He gently jostled her shoulder. She groaned again before her eyes fluttered open. Her fingers found their way to her head.

"Careful. You're bleeding," he said.

"I am?" She tried to shift in her seat, then winced and grew still. Her eyes slammed shut. She swallowed hard. "Wh-what happened? Where are we?"

"We had kind of a rough landing. Now we're upside down in the middle of a field. The good news is you landed."

Her eyes opened. "Landed where?"

He leaned close, surveying her face. Yeah, one pupil was definitely dilated. Wasn't that the main sign of a concussion?

"You told me a little while ago that this is the Knutsen property. Except he isn't home right now."

Her brows slanted. She slowly turned her head sideways, then grimaced. "That's…not possible. He lives in the middle of nowhere."

Oh, boy. Panic squeezed his lungs. His pulse sped as he looked around. This was not good.

He had basic first-aid skills, but what was he supposed to do about a head injury?

"Does your head hurt?"

She gave an almost imperceptible nod. "It hurts a lot."

"Can you look at me?"

Her troubled gaze found his. Tears welled. He reached over and squeezed her hand. Her fingers were like icicles. "You're going to be okay. We'll figure this out."

"I'm so sorry." Her lower lip trembled. "This is all my fault."

"No, it's not." He caressed the back of her hand with his thumb. "We're both alive and that's what matters. I'm going to get us out of here."

Okay, that was a ridiculous notion. He could tend to that cut on her forehead and get her a bottle of water from his backpack, but they were still officially stranded. "Are you feeling sick to your stomach?"

"My stomach?" She frowned. "No. Why?"

"I thought when people hit their head, they sometimes felt nauseous. Never mind." Sam dragged his hand down his face. "I'm not a pilot or a health care professional. Pretend I didn't say that."

A soft smile tipped up one corner of her mouth. "You're funny today, Sam Frazier."

"Well, I'm glad you think so."

And at least she knew who he was, so that had to count for something, right?

"Here, hold this on that cut on your forehead." He folded a T-shirt he'd found inside her bag into a square and gently pressed it against the gash. "I'm going to try and call for help on the radio."

She winced again, but took his advice and placed the cloth over her wound.

He grabbed the walkie-talkie from her bag, twisted the knob, then squeezed the button on the side. "Mayday. Mayday. This is Sam Frazier and Rylee Madden. We're crash landed in Mr. Knutsen's field. Orca Island in Alaska. Can anyone hear me?"

He released the button on the transmitter. Only static greeted him.

Rylee's body shook as she laughed quietly.

Irritation prickled. He set the walkie-talkie down. "I'm glad you think this is amusing."

She snorted, then sucked in a breath. "I'm sorry. You just…that was super cute."

If she weren't bleeding and injured, he'd have a few choice words to share with her right now. An acrid odor tinged his nostrils and he sniffed the air. "Do you smell that?"

Rylee pulled the shirt from her cut and turned her head slowly from side to side. "Smells like pizza. No, that's not right. Can't find my words," she mumbled.

His heart pounded. "We've got to get out."

"Get out of here? But I like it." She snuggled into her seat. "Feels cozy."

"Something's burning, Rylee. We're on fire. Come on, let's go." He fumbled with her safety belt. Thankfully, it gave way and he was able to pull Rylee against him.

"Wow, you're strong." She patted his chest awkwardly with her hand. "But how are we going to move if you're hugging me?"

"I haven't figured that out yet. But we don't have much time."

"Don't panic, Sam." Rylee's eyes fluttered closed. "You've got this."

"I am panicking. If this plane catches on fire with us inside, we'll be trapped."

His words must've registered because her eyes flew open and she tried to push away. He held her close. "We're upside down. Be careful."

She whimpered in pain. "My arm. It hurts like my head."

Please, God. *No.* A broken arm, a concussion and a fire? He forced his features not to betray the fear simmering inside him. "Listen. Here's what's going to happen. You'll stay close and

I'm going to slowly scootch toward the door and get us out. Ready?"

"Scootching is good," she said. "I like to scootch."

"As soon as I get you out, I'll need to grab as much survival gear as possible."

"Survival gear. Hmm." Her face twisted into another frown. "Check the cargo hold maybe."

He guided them toward the door and quickly surveyed the back of the plane behind his seat. The smell was getting worse. Smoke curled through the air outside the plane's windows. "Do you have a fire extinguisher?"

"Hope so." She braced her injured arm against her chest. "Those are super important for our Super Cub."

Oh, my. She was just plain loopy at this point. His mind raced. How could he get her safely outside without causing further harm?

Somehow, he managed to exit the aircraft and settle her on the ground a safe distance away. Using his jacket for a temporary face covering, he stumbled, coughing, through the smoke and back toward the plane. His eyes stung as he crawled through the interior. He found one small bag with snacks and a red duffel with a First Aid label on the outside. He grabbed his backpack and her tote bag, plus two bottles of water. If there was a fire extinguisher on board, he couldn't find it.

By the time he made it back to Rylee's side, black smoke filled the air. She sat on the ground, cradling her arm against her chest. He could already see that her forearm was curving in an unnatural angle. Coughing, he set everything he'd rescued on the ground beside Rylee, then glanced back at the plane. Red and orange flames licked at the base of the aircraft's fuselage. They had to find a safe place to shelter. Even with the rain that had moved through, it might not be enough moisture to stop the fire from spreading. This meadow full of grass would go up in flames in a matter of minutes.

"I'm going to look for another fire extinguisher."

She lifted one shoulder in a helpless shrug.

He didn't wait for a response. Turning away, he jogged toward the closest building. A windowless shed with a sturdy door. Sam jiggled the doorknob. Locked.

"What do I do?"

He spun in a circle then sprinted across the yard to the house. His boots pounded up the steps and he rapped on the door. "Anyone here? Hello? Please help."

Nothing.

Sam tried the knob and rammed his shoulder against the door. It barely budged under the force of his weight. The place was locked down tight.

Defeated, he left the porch and trudged back to Rylee. The flames crackled, mocking him. Bits of ash floated into the air. His efforts had done nothing. They were going to lose the plane. Now they were officially stranded in the middle of nowhere.

He never should've come to Hearts Bay.

Chapter Twelve

"What if no one finds us?" Rylee whispered.

Her head wasn't pounding quite so much, and she no longer saw two of Sam when she looked at him. The pain in her arm had almost become bearable. But now she had the capacity to evaluate their circumstances.

And she was terrified.

Sam turned from where he stood in the entrance of their makeshift shelter. Tugging on the rope he'd found somewhere near the Knutsen house, he readjusted the blue tarp he'd fashioned into a barrier from the weather. And the mosquitoes. The swarm had descended. Rylee had used her uninjured arm to swat the pests away.

They'd been huddled in a lean-to structure built beside a cluster of tall pine trees several yards from the property's main house for hours.

The stench from the burning plane still wafted toward them. A tendril of smoke curled up from the wreckage.

"If any good can come from this, maybe the fire might help someone spot us." Sam sat down beside her and draped a thermal blanket over their legs. She only could recall bits and pieces of their misadventure. The last thing she did remember was banking the plane over the coastline to show him the orcas. Sam had patiently answered her questions, filling in the gaps in her memory. He'd guided her to the safety of this structure away from the wreckage.

"I knocked on the door of the house and the small cabin behind it again. No one answered. There's an ax in the carport, and I was half tempted to break in, but…"

Rylee shook her head. "We're not that desperate."

Yet. There was no need to break in and trespass on Mr. Knutsen's property. They were safe for now in this shelter that doubled as a firewood storage shed. But with the mosquitoes buzzing around, the throbbing pain of her injuries, and more clouds blanketing the remote part of Orca Island, she was starting to crack.

"We'll get through this." Sam tipped his head back against a pile of wood that was nearly stacked to the roof of the shed.

Hot tears stung the backs of her eyes. She'd tried so hard all afternoon to be brave. Strong. But she couldn't keep pretending. Not to mention her head felt like it was full of Jell-O and she could barely string together three coherent sentences before she was exhausted and needed a nap. "This is all my fault." She used the back of her hand to swipe at the moisture dripping from her nose. Being stranded out here in the wilderness had given her the freedom to let go of basic manners. "I should have known better than to bring you out here. I wanted to show you the beauty of the island."

"Aww, come here." Sam stretched out one arm. She hesitated, then leaned against him, her head pressed against his firm chest. "This is not your fault. It's an accident, and you did your best."

"No, I didn't." Her pathetic tears dampened his sweatshirt. "I was showing off, trying to impress you. The pod was so beautiful to follow. Then I thought I'd show you how well I could maneuver the aircraft in this canyon. The truth is I knew better. Weather changes quickly out here and the topography is challenging. I should have turned around and gone back to Hearts Bay as soon as I saw those clouds on the horizon."

Sam's chest rose and fell beneath her cheek

as he breathed in and out. No doubt processing her confession. What a thing to admit to the man who'd been about to acquire her employer's business. Had her carelessness influenced the outcome of the acquisition? Her blood ran cold. Paul and Libby would never forgive her if she'd botched this. They wanted desperately to relocate. If Frazier backed out, they'd have to find a new buyer and maybe even postpone their move to Nevada.

"Hey. Listen." Sam pulled away slightly. His gaze dipped, warming her skin. She forced herself to make eye contact. He used the pad of his thumb to gently wipe away the tears on her cheeks. It was so foolish to let her guard down like this, but she couldn't help leaning in to his touch.

Empathy filled his eyes. "You're being too hard on yourself, Rylee. This could've been so much worse. What if you'd been forced to ditch the aircraft over water? We're fortunate that we're not burned or dealing with life-threatening injuries. You're an excellent pilot. Someone's going to find us soon. God's got this. You'll see."

She wanted to believe him. Oh, how she wished she could have that certainty he clung to. But her head hurt and every time she moved her arm, the pain zinged up to her shoulders.

Bouts of nausea and ringing in her ears added to the misery. And the rain had returned with a vengeance. Her beloved plane was nothing more than a cooked shell. Sure, they'd survive the night, but it was going to be rough.

"I'm so sorry, Sam. To think that I could have…" She trailed off. The words died on her lips. She couldn't possibly finish the sentence. Her impulsivity could've gotten them both killed.

"If you're thinking of Silas, don't worry. He's in good hands. We've got to try to stay positive. Your injuries are treatable, and I'm a little banged up, but we're going to be fine. We'll figure this out together. When we don't show up tonight, I'm confident your family will take action."

Despite their dire circumstances, Sam's words offered an inkling of hope. They could most definitely rely on her family and the people of Hearts Bay to launch a search party. Her parents wouldn't rest until she and Sam were safe.

How had he been so foolish? Sam winced as he pushed to a seated position, his stiff body protesting from a night spent on the hard ground. That question had needled him throughout the night as he'd struggled to sleep.

Now that he was wide-awake, he couldn't keep batting away the truth. He'd carelessly overlooked God's gracious provision. The Lord had placed an incredible woman right in his path, and Sam had been too preoccupied with his own agenda to notice. Or maybe he'd just been too scared to admit that Rylee was everything he needed and wanted in a partner.

He turned and glanced down at Rylee, who had fallen asleep on the ground, a backpack wedged under her head for her pillow. Should he wake her? During their first few hours after the accident, he'd tried to stay alert. Checked on her and woken her whenever she'd slept for more than ninety minutes. But that had quickly exhausted them both. Even though birds chirped nearby and the storm had passed, for now he'd let her rest.

He scrubbed his hand across his face, then assessed their meager options for breakfast. Rylee hadn't been very hungry yesterday, but he'd still been careful about not eating more than his share of the can of cashews, or the four energy bars and two apples he'd found in her bag. He was reaching for an apple when the distant whine of an airplane caught his attention.

He'd never claimed to be an expert on aviation. Far from it, really. The drone of those twin propellers spinning was hard to miss, though. Adrenaline surged through his veins. He scrambled toward the entrance, shoving the tarp out of his way. The familiar sound drew his attention upward. He got to his feet, stumbled, then regained his footing. The white plane with yellow stripes was a welcome sight against the pale blue backdrop of a cloudless sky. He squinted in the early morning sunlight and rushed out into the middle of the field, waving his hands overhead. "Hey! Hey, look down here."

The plane soared overhead.

"No, please come back. Lord, please make them turn around." He kept waving. Surely, they'd seen him? Or noticed the wreckage of a burned-out plane smoldering on the ground? He jogged a few steps on the uneven terrain, determined to flag them down. "Come on. Don't you see me over here? Help!" The plane banked to the right, made a slow lap over the Knutsen property, then dipped its wing.

Sam sucked in a breath. Did the pilot plan on landing or what? Sam stared into the sky, one palm braced over his eyes to shield from the sun. The pilot dipped the other wing, flying slightly lower.

"Oh, thank You, God." That had to be some

sort of signal. The wing tipping. Maybe the universal sign of acknowledgment?

But then the plane climbed higher and flew away.

"No. No, no, no, no." Sam jogged a few paces. "Come back. Please!"

How could that be? When the plane disappeared and the engine noise faded, Sam turned and trudged back to the shed. Dejected. He wasn't even clever enough to get them rescued. From the moment he'd sensed trouble during their flight yesterday, all he'd done was ask questions. He'd second-guessed Rylee's decisions and made his doubts and frustrations crystal clear.

Worse, she'd been in crisis mode and he'd done very little to help except push the airplane into position for takeoff. Sure, at the last minute, he'd found the gumption to carry her from the burning plane. But only because he'd been absolutely terrified of losing her.

Terrified of losing her.

His brain circled around that phrase. Reexamined the words. Held the notion up to the light. When it came right down to it, a life-or-death situation had made him realize what mattered. But now she had a concussion, a broken arm, and they may have just missed their opportunity to be rescued. Now was not the time to talk about their future. If they even had a future. The poor girl didn't make sense half the time when she spoke. It wasn't fair to ask her to have a vulnerable conversation.

He quietly pulled back the tarp and stepped inside the shelter. Rylee opened her eyes and sat up, cradling her arm to her chest. The makeshift sling they'd pulled together, along with the aluminum splint from the emergency supplies, kept her arm from moving. But, man, she looked like she was in pain.

"What's going on? Is it morning?"

"Yeah." Sam sank back onto the ground beside her. "Somebody just flew over. I tried to flag them down, but they kept going."

She gasped. "Wait, what? Somebody flew by?"

He nodded. "White plane with yellow stripes. Loud engine. Twin propellers. Why do you think they didn't land?"

"If the pilot didn't circle back around and try again, maybe they'll come back. Might need fuel, or they saw that we'd crashed so they just went ahead and alerted the Coast Guard. It's good that they spotted us."

"I hope they send help soon." He rummaged in his bag for an energy bar. They had two left. "Breakfast? You can have the peanut butter. I'll take the honey oat."

"Thanks." Her mouth hitched up in a smile, but he could see the pain and fatigue in her eyes.

Less than an hour later, a different sound filled the quiet air. The steady thump, thump, thump of a helicopter's rotors.

Rylee's eyes widened as her gaze found his. "Do you hear that?"

"Sure do." He hurried out of the shed and back into the field. The bright orange-and-white copter hovered overhead, a uniformed figure in the open doorway.

"Hey!" Sam waved his arms. "Down here."

A man's voice came through the megaphone. "We see you, sir. Lowering the basket now."

"Rylee." Sam turned and raced back to the shed. "Rylee, it's the Coast Guard. They're here and they've got a basket."

A few minutes later, a basket and a man in a uniform zipped down as the helicopter hovered.

Sam fell to his knees, blinking back tears. "Thank You, Lord."

"Oh, good. You're awake."

Rylee turned her head toward the sound of her sister Tess's familiar voice. "Hey."

Tess stood inside the door of Rylee's room at Hearts Bay Community Hospital. "How are you feeling?"

Rylee tried sitting up in bed, winced, then changed her mind. "Better, I guess."

Tess's gray canvas slip-on shoes squeaked against the linoleum as she crossed the room. Her dark hair was twisted into a bun and she wore a gray-and-white-striped scoop-necked T-shirt and faded denim cut-off shorts. "Let me help you sit up."

"Okay." Yawning, Rylee glanced out the window. The bright sunlight streaming through the open blinds confused her. "What time is it? What day is it?"

"You've been here for about a day. It's Thursday afternoon." Tess found the gray plastic remote under Rylee's sheet and pressed the button. Slowly, the back of the bed raised a few inches.

"Can I get you anything?"

"Something to drink would be great."

"No problem. I'll be right back. Oh, and there's someone here who'd like to see you."

"What? Tess, no." Ignoring Rylee's protest, Tess slipped out the door.

Rylee dragged her fingers through her tangled hair, glanced down at her scratchy pale pink hospital gown and the fiberglass cast adorning her right arm. There wasn't a mirror anywhere around, but she must look hideous. And she didn't smell very good, either.

"Please let this be a family member," she whispered.

The door opened and Sam stepped in. He, of course, looked incredible, minus the dark circles under his eyes. He'd shaved and was wearing jeans, sneakers and a dark green hoodie. Worry flitted across his features. "Hey." His voice was deep and smooth. Their gazes locked. Butterflies took flight in her abdomen.

"Hi." She managed to find the word. "How are you?"

"I'm all right. Still a little sore. You?"

"I have a cool cast." She gestured to her arm. "If you can find a marker, I'll let you sign it."

His smile didn't quite meet his eyes. "I'd be honored. How's your head?"

"Better, I suppose. I feel more like myself."

She still didn't remember everything that had happened. A fresh wave of embarrassment crested inside. How much ridiculous stuff had she said to him, anyway?

"Is it okay if I stay for a few minutes?"

Yes. No. Warmth heated her skin. Why did this feel so awkward?

"Come on in." She tried for a smile. But there was something about the tension in his jaw. The uncertainty lingering in the air made her nervous. She twisted the bedsheet around her fingers. "Where is Silas?"

"With a babysitter. When her family found out what had happened, they offered to do whatever they could. Between them and your parents, Silas is getting plenty of attention."

"Oh, good. I'm glad. Would you like to sit down?" She gestured to the blue recliner in the corner next to her bed.

"No, I think I'd better stand."

Her heart turned over. He moved closer, then stopped beside her bed and reached for her hand. "Rylee, listen. There's something important I need to say."

Oh, this wasn't good. How long had she been asleep? Why did he sound so serious?

"Our unexpected adventure gave me a lot to think about. Seeing Josh and Crystal get married, and since losing my brother and my sister-in-law, I've learned an important lesson this summer. It's that life is short. We're not guaranteed anything. And I know this is so sudden, I mean we've only known each other for less than a month, but I've fallen in love with you."

Her breath caught. "What?"

"I know this is an unconventional place to share my feelings, but I can't go another day without telling you the truth. Ever since you scooped Silas out of his car seat when we first got here that day at the airport, I've been captivated. Not just by your kindness, either. You're intelligent and beautiful and so very brave."

"Sam, please, I don't—"

He gently squeezed her hand. "Please let me finish before I lose my confidence. I don't want to be without you, Rylee. Silas and I need you in our lives."

Her head throbbed. Was this a dream? He couldn't mean it. Not after she'd been so careless and nearly killed them in a plane crash. "Sam, what are you…? What are you saying?"

His smile evaporated. "I'm in love with you, Rylee. I don't want us to be apart. Obviously, Silas is my priority now, and dating a guy that is responsible for a baby maybe isn't what you had expected, but I'm really hoping that you'll give me an opportunity. Give us an opportunity."

She pulled her hand from his. "You live in Seattle. You've already told me how much you want to make sure people in other countries have clean water."

His brow furrowed. "How is that relevant to our relationship?"

"Because I live here. My family is here. My everything is here. I can't just uproot and move."

Hurt pinched his features. "I guess I thought you'd consider visiting me. At first."

She blinked back tears. "And then what, Sam? I'll suddenly change my mind and give up my life here because what you have to offer in Seattle is so incredible?"

Sam stuffed his hands in the front pocket of his hoodie. His wounded gaze roamed her face. "Yes, that's what I'd hoped. It's not out of the question, is it? You coming to Seattle? People pack up and move for relationships all the time. I mean Seattle's a big change, but you'd adjust. Eventually. You'd find a new job in a no time."

"Why do I have to move? Why can't you and Silas move here? Isn't the acquisition still happening?"

"I never said I'd stay on with Frazier just because we acquired Hearts Bay Aviation." Sam's clipped words made her angry. "In fact, I was quite honest about my plans for leaving the company."

"And I've been quite honest about my plans to stay on the island."

A thorny silence filled the space between them.

"I guess I was hoping you'd be willing to reconsider."

"Yeah, well, we've had a lot of fun together and Silas is adorable. But I can't leave this island. I *won't* leave this island. At least, not permanently. I'm truly sorry if I gave you the impression that I would. Please. Go back to Seattle. It's where you belong."

"Rylee, I…"

"I'm not changing my mind."

His Adam's apple bobbed up and down as he swallowed hard. "All right, if that's how you feel. I appreciate your honesty. Take care."

"Goodbye, Sam."

He turned and walked away.

As soon as the door closed, she let the tears slide down her cheeks. Tess returned and Rylee quickly wiped her fingers across her face. Her sister stopped just inside the door, holding a disposable cup with a lid and a straw. "Oh, no. What have you done?"

Chapter Thirteen

Sam sat in his home office in Seattle, tapping a pencil eraser against a blank yellow notepad. His laptop sat open beside him on his desk, but he had no interest in working.

For at least the tenth time in the last hour, his gaze wandered to the window. A light drizzle fell from a granite-gray sky. The leaves on the aspen tree in his yard had started turning a brilliant shade of gold. One of his favorite milestones that marked the arrival of fall.

Except this year, he found no joy in admiring the stately tree.

Out in the den, Silas babbled away, probably captivating both sets of grandparents. Since the memorial service two weeks ago, Erin's parents had stayed in town. It had been awkward at first, dealing with his parents and hers, all vying for time with their grandson. Expressing their opinions and questioning his childcare arrangements.

Slowly, they'd each come to an understanding about what Silas needed. They hadn't approved of all the plans and routines Sam had implemented since he and Silas had returned from Alaska a month ago, but after more than a few tense discussions, they'd reached a more peaceful place. He'd patiently explained his reasons for how he took care of Silas, and they'd come to understand and respect his rationale. It took effort on everyone's part, but Erin's parents and Sam's mother and father recognized that parenting for him, as a single dad, would look different than their own experiences.

His inbox filled with six more messages. His exhale blew away the strain from the day and he closed the laptop lid. Coming back home was supposed to make him happy. Fulfilled. The acquisition was all wrapped up. Hearts Bay Aviation had been officially acquired. Despite all his doubts and the messy struggle, he'd managed to do his part.

And he'd never felt lonelier or more dissatisfied.

No matter how often he hiked or went for a jog, met with his friends, or listened to Silas jabber, his thoughts just circled back to Rylee. Was she healthy? Had her symptoms resolved?

A new general manager had been hired to oversee operations on Orca Island. Sam had double-checked with him to make sure Rylee was back at work. She certainly wasn't responding to his text messages. He didn't intend to try again. He'd have to give her space. That seemed to be what she wanted. Even though it was the opposite of what he wanted.

"Son? Do you have a few minutes?"

Sam swiveled in his chair. His dad stood in the doorway, hands tucked in his khaki-colored pants' pockets. He wore a brown sweater layered over a collared shirt.

"Is Silas okay?" Sam rose halfway from his chair. "I lost track of time. Does he need to eat?"

Dad smiled and motioned for him to sit back down. "Both of his grandmothers are analyzing the kid's every move. Rest assured he has more than enough attention."

Sam reclaimed his seat. "What's on your mind, Dad?"

"You haven't quite been yourself since you got home. Your mother and I thought it was the dread of your brother and Erin's memorial service, but it's been two weeks and you're still moping. What gives?"

Sam dragged his palm across his face. He saw no reason to obfuscate. "I met someone in Hearts Bay. I thought the feeling was mutual, but I learned the hard way that she is not interested."

Empathy filled his father's eyes. "I'm sorry to hear that. After everything you've been through this summer, that's quite a blow."

A pang struck his middle and Sam looked away, fidgeting with a flash drive sitting on his desk.

Dad cleared his throat. "I appreciate everything you've done. That acquisition had its challenges, and we're fortunate that you were able to perform at a high level, especially with Silas in tow."

Whoa. He had not expected such high praise. "I was more than happy to help."

"So, would you consider relocating to Hearts Bay?"

Sam stared at his father, wondering if he'd heard him correctly. This seemed completely out of the blue. His dad hadn't even hinted at this possibility in all their dealings so far. He'd thought things were running smoothly with the acquired company.

"Why? You just hired a general manager."

Dad shook his head. "Not going to work long-term. He's already asked when he can transfer back. Evidently his wife's concerned about the winter weather."

Sam couldn't stop a smile. "That's unfortunate. Seems like something a person would research before they accepted the role."

"Agreed." Dad settled into a chair opposite Sam's desk and rubbed his palms against his pant legs. "I've got to be honest, Sam, we need someone trustworthy and reliable on that island."

"I can't argue with that."

"You know, for a guy who claims not to care much about aviation, you poured yourself into seeing that merger through." Dad hesitated. His gaze found Sam's. "I'm proud of you."

Sam's throat thickened. He cleared his throat. "Thank you."

"This person that you met? Did she light the spark that motivated you to work hard?"

"She's part of the reason. My friend Brandt sent me that article in the newspaper about our family and I got so angry. The skepticism, questioning your integrity as a leader, implications that we couldn't survive. None of it was accurate. I was determined to prove to you, to myself, and to everyone that I could do what I was asked to do."

Dad nodded. "Uh-huh. I see. So this person that you met, did you have something to prove to her?"

"I don't know. Maybe." Sam tucked the flash

drive in his desk. "She's stubborn. There will be no moving her off that island."

"Then maybe you need to move there."

Again, Sam was surprised by his father. The man was usually all business and he didn't meddle in personal matters.

Sam shook his head. "She was adamant that things weren't going to work out between us."

"Is she someone worth fighting for?"

"Absolutely. But I'm committed to these wells and helping people in Nicaragua. If I go back to Alaska, I'm concerned I won't be able to keep things running smoothly in the villages."

"Maybe it's time you hire someone more qualified."

"More qualified than who?"

Dad huffed out a long breath. "You're making this more difficult than it needs to be. You gave your heart away, son. That's more important than any business achievement. Above all else, your mother and I want you to be happy, to live a fulfilling life and have a strong relationship with the Lord. That's what matters most."

Sam's jaw hung open.

"I've failed you in many ways, Sam. Losing your brother is a stark reminder to all of us not to neglect our loved ones."

Sam found his voice. "What are you really asking me?"

"I'm asking you not to walk away from Frazier Aviation, or from someone you care deeply about. Don't let her get away."

Sam drummed his fingers on the table. He could hardly believe his father was being so sensitive, pushing him toward a nonbusiness decision. But maybe this was God at work in his heart. Maybe his father had come to understand how important life outside of an office was. "All right. I'll consider going back to Hearts Bay. On one condition."

"What's that?"

"You let me hire the general manager."

Dad's craggy features broke into a smile. "Do you have someone in mind?"

"Absolutely."

That had been the longest six weeks of her life.

Rylee gently flexed and extended her wrist. It was a little sore, but that wouldn't stop her from enjoying her first meal without that dumb cast.

Dr. Rasmussen had removed her cast and x-rayed her arm during her appointment today, then proclaimed her officially healed. She'd need physical therapy and a few more weeks of light duty at work before she could hop back in a plane's cockpit, though.

Fragments of memories from her flight with Sam flickered through her head. She still couldn't recall every detail, but with each week that passed, her brain served up more information. Dr. Rasmussen had assured her that was all part of a normal recovery after a concussion.

Maybe she'd never remember all the details. Maybe that was God's grace for her. To be honest, the less she thought about Sam Frazier, the less her heart hurt.

Conversation ebbed and flowed as she ate dinner with her whole family, including Grandmother. They'd gathered around her parents' table to celebrate the end of her cast and her sister Eliana's last night in town before she went back to Idaho with her family.

Rylee tucked into the baked halibut caught fresh today when Eliana's husband, Tate, had gone fishing with their brother-in-law, Asher. They'd caught a two-hundred-and-seventy-five-pound halibut and helped fill the freezers of plenty of folks around town.

Rylee took a bite and closed her eyes, savoring the fresh fish baked in a buttery dill cream sauce. The crisp green beans, Mia's homemade dinner rolls and the berry cobbler cooling on the rack nearby rounded out a scrumptious meal.

"Hey, what's that?"

Rylee opened her eyes and looked around. Poppy, Gus's daughter, pointed to a toy Molly Jo held in her hand. Rylee's mouth went dry. Conversation around the table sputtered. Molly Jo grinned from her spot on Heath's lap, clearly thrilled to be the center of attention.

Rylee stopped chewing. Molly Jo banged the plastic rattle against Heath's outstretched hand, jiggling the rainbow beads inside. The swooshing sound inside the plastic ball reminded her of Silas and Molly Jo playing together on Lexi and Heath's floor.

"That was a toy Silas was playing with," Rylee said softly.

People shifted in their seats and exchanged knowing glances.

"Mine," Molly Jo insisted, and shook the rattle again.

"Well, you should give it back," Poppy said.

Rylee looked down at her food. "Maybe we could mail it to him."

Her sister Tess reached over and gently squeezed her shoulder. "That's tough when memories come at you like that, isn't it?"

"No big deal." Rylee cut her off and forced a smile.

Tess studied her, then went back to eating.

Rylee stabbed at a green bean with her fork.

She had to get used to talking about Silas and Sam. The Fraziers had acquired Hearts Bay Aviation. Paul and Libby had moved, and a new operations manager had taken over. She and Carson had texted quite a bit. Carson wasn't happy, but he was trying to stay positive.

She didn't plan on seeing Sam or Silas again. That was the problem. Thoughts of not seeing them again made her chest ache. She'd cried buckets of tears since Sam had walked out of her hospital room.

How in the world would she ever move on?

"Have you heard from him at all?" Mom asked.

"No." Rylee picked up her glass of iced tea. "I don't know why I would."

"This halibut is incredible, Mom," Eliana said. "Mine never tastes like yours when I try this recipe."

Mom shrugged. "I make it the same way every time. No secrets."

"Sam seemed like a really nice guy," Lexi said. "I hate that things didn't work out."

A headache pressed against Rylee's forehead.

"He hasn't texted you to see if you've recovered?" Mia frowned. "That doesn't seem like him."

"Maybe you could apologize," Tess suggested. "Make the first move."

"Yeah, tell him you've had a change of heart." Eliana passed the breadbasket to Lexi. "May I have the butter, please?"

Rylee took a long sip of tea, then eyed her sisters. "What should I apologize for, Tess? Not wanting to traipse off to Seattle when I've built a life here?" She sighed. "Can't a girl just eat her first meal cast-free in peace?"

"Sure. We'll wait until you finish your dessert," Lexi teased.

"But then we're going to talk about this because you've been moping around here for weeks." Mia leveled her most disapproving look. "It's not healthy."

"News flash, I survived a plane crash and had a broken arm. Grounded, remember?"

"But from what I've heard, you told Sam to go away." Eliana slathered butter on her dinner roll and shot her a pointed look.

Oh, brother. Heat flooded Rylee's cheeks. "Is this an intervention?"

"Do you need one?" Eliana asked.

"What I need is for all of you to mind your own business." Rylee shoved her chair away from the table. "I'm going to get some air."

Eliana had only been back in town for a week. How could she possibly know what went on with Sam? Guilt and anger battled for position as Rylee strode toward the door and slipped outside.

The crisp September air made her instantly regret not grabbing a jacket. She was too stubborn to go back in and get one, though. Carefully, she wrapped her arms around her torso and walked into her parents' yard.

As much as she hated to admit that her family was right, Sam's departure from the island had crushed her. He'd texted her a few times, sure, but she'd not been ready to respond, and eventually he'd stopped.

He seemed like a really nice guy. I hate that it didn't work out.

Of all the unsolicited opinions, Lexi's observation played on repeat.

Pushing him away was not the best choice. But was she ready to admit that to anyone? Not tonight. Not in front of her entire family.

Except, what if she'd waited too long and he'd moved on?

The thought of him meeting someone new, then introducing her to Silas, and eventually creating a life with another woman made her want to weep. See? That was the problem. She walked around the side of the house and into the backyard.

She'd been trying not to worry. Trying not to think about him. But every time she turned around, there was something that took her back. Like tonight, with Molly Jo holding one of Silas's toys. Or walking past the park where they'd had lunch. Or that place overlooking the harbor where they'd shared their first kiss. She could not escape reminders of Sam. Not even here in her parents' yard, a few feet from where they'd talked and laughed on the Fourth of July.

Her efforts to protect her heart had failed miserably. In the end, he'd won her over with his kindness and his charm. But now she had no idea what to do. Were her sisters right? Was she supposed to reach out and apologize? And for what? She couldn't say she was sorry she loved her life here, loved being near her family. That would be a lie.

The familiar hum of an approaching plane drew her attention to the evening sky. Wow. They were flying low and slow.

"Wait a second," she said. "That's Carson's plane."

He'd texted an hour ago to see if she'd been cleared by the doctor to return to work. He hadn't said anything about an evening flight-seeing trip. Maybe he'd picked up a walk-in customer at the last minute. Orca Island had been blessed with a gorgeous extended summer. There hadn't been much rain. Tourists had been traveling to the island regularly, squeezing in their last trip before fall officially arrived. She was about to go back inside and face her exuberant family when she spotted the banner trailing behind the plane.

Okay. That was weird. Carson definitely would've bragged about getting to tow a banner. They rarely got those requests.

Then she read the banner's words and her face warmed.

"'I love you, Rylee,'" she read out loud under her breath. What? Was this a joke? No, it wasn't. A filament of hope sparked inside.

The plane banked and turned around, then flew by again. She waved both arms overhead. He tipped his wings from side to side. The banner snapped and popped in the wind.

The back door opened and her family filed out. Even Grandmother. They all stared with expectant smiles.

"Did you know about this?" She pointed to the plane, making another slow loop over the bay.

"Yep." Dad smiled proudly. "What do you think?"

"I don't know what to think." She pressed her palms to her cheeks. "Is it from Sam? I mean I hope it's from Sam. Unless it's from all of you, which would be really sweet, but—"

"Rylee, go into the front yard," Heath said.

"What's going on?" Her pulse sped. She glanced at Mom. "Are you feeling well?"

"Never better, honey. Thanks for asking. Do you want us to film a video?"

"Mom." Eliana shot her an exasperated look. "Not another word."

"Rylee. If you don't go around to the front of the house, we will carry you there ourselves," Mia said, pointing. "Go. Please. You have to trust us."

"But I can see the plane just fine from here," she insisted.

Mia released a protracted groan. "Stubborn, stubborn girl. Please go stand in the driveway."

"All right. Fine. I'm going now." Rylee turned and strode toward the driveway. They could really be so bossy sometimes. Why didn't they just tell her who had ordered the banner? She rounded the corner of the house. Sam stood in the middle of the yard holding a gorgeous bouquet of flowers.

She stopped and clapped her hand over her mouth. Tears stung her eyes.

He offered a tentative smile. "Hi."

She let her arms fall to her sides. "What are you doing here?"

"I heard there was going to be an air show tonight. A special request from an out-of-towner who's crazy about this local pilot."

Nervous laughter burst from her lips. She took slow, careful steps toward him. "Did you have something to do with that banner?"

His tender gaze roamed her face. "Do you want me to be responsible for that banner?"

She nodded, stopping inches away from him.

"Good, because it was from me. These are for you as well." He held out the bouquet of red roses, pink carnations and brilliant lilies.

"Thank you." The plastic crinkled as she held the flowers in her arms and breathed in deep. They smelled good. "I—I can't believe you're here."

"Rylee, I—"

"I'm so sorry, Sam." Her voice broke. "I was terribly ashamed of what happened. The way I botched that flight and cartwheeled the plane. So humiliating. I just couldn't bring myself to let you care about me."

The words tumbled out in a rush. The lightness she felt from speaking the truth finally rivaled anything she'd ever felt in the air. She couldn't hold the tears back anymore.

"Oh, sweetheart." Sam reached up and cupped her face with his hands. "No one blames you. That was an unfortunate situation that could've happened to any pilot. Please, let go of that burden."

"I want to," she whispered, more tears blurring her vision. "My pride got in the way. It nearly destroyed us before we barely got started."

"I think my pride was involved too." His grin stretched wide. "But you're willing to admit that there's an us?"

Laughter burst through her tears. "I hope so. I mean you just paid for a flyover with a banner."

His expression grew serious. "You're right. I did. Because I love you with my whole heart and I wanted to tell the world."

"I love you too."

He caressed her cheeks with his thumbs. "May I kiss you?"

"I thought you'd never ask."

Angling his head to one side, Sam closed the distance between them and claimed her mouth with his. An enthusiastic whoop went up from inside the house.

Rylee pulled away just long enough to grimace. "I'm so sorry that we have an audience."

Sam's heavy-lidded gaze made her knees weak. "Don't be. Your family made this reunion possible."

"In that case, let's give them something to talk about."

Sam dipped her low and kissed her again.

Epilogue

One year later

She'd never let herself daydream about this part. It had always been too painful to think about. A dream that only came true for her sisters and closest friends.

Until Sam Frazier proposed last Christmas Eve.

Now, in just a few minutes, she would walk down the aisle and become his wife.

"You look stunning, Rylee." She met her mother's gaze in the mirror of the church classroom set up as the bride's dressing room.

"Thank you, Mom."

Rylee turned from side to side, admiring her reflection. The full skirt with the tiny flowers appliquéd on the long train, along with the elegant sleeveless design and fitted bodice, was not the kind of dress she'd ever envisioned.

Until she'd met Sam.

Before he'd walked into her life, she'd accepted that wearing white and floating down the center aisle of the church where she'd grown up maybe wouldn't be God's plan for her.

But slowly Sam's love and God's faithfulness had healed those broken wounded places. The Lord had used Sam's tender kindness, his loyalty and his patience to show her a love she hadn't believed possible.

Mom reached up and gently checked that the sparkly tiara was clipped in place. Then she adjusted the long gauzy veil, fluffing the end around Rylee's bare shoulders.

"Come on, sweetie. Your dad and a church full of people who love you are waiting."

Her heart pounding, Rylee left the classroom and went out into the hallway. Dad met her and offered his arm.

"You're gorgeous, Rylee." He kissed her cheek. "Sam is a fortunate fella."

"Thank you, Dad. I love you."

His proud expression made her want to weep. "I love you too."

The wedding coordinator had put Annie in charge of keeping Molly Jo, Poppy and Silas in line. Bless Annie's heart. She was pulling double duty as a bridesmaid and wrangler of small children. Together, the children were supposed to carry the ring bearer's pillow and sprinkle flower petals down the aisle.

Rylee couldn't hold back a laugh. Lucy, Molly Jo and Poppy in their adorable flower girl dresses, and Silas in his dapper gray suit, were a sight to behold. Rylee had invited all her nieces and nephews to be a part of the wedding. She'd offered to have one of the bridesmaids bring Lexi and Heath's baby boy, Cade, and Gus and Mia's newborn, Kayla, down the aisle in a double stroller, but Lexi had convinced her that would be a bit much. Now that she saw how much effort Annie had to invest in keeping three little ones focused, she had to admit Lexi had been right.

Her sisters, all dressed in simple blue bridesmaids' dresses and holding gorgeous bouquets, lined up in front of Annie outside the doors to the sanctuary. Mia glanced back, met Rylee's gaze and smiled through her tears.

"We added this while you were getting ready," Dad said, his voice thick with unshed tears. He pointed to framed photos displayed next to the guest book and a bouquet of lilies on a table nearby.

"Oh, my." A lump rose in Rylee's throat. Her brother, Charlie, stood on the dock beside their grandfather. In the background, she recognized Grandpa's fishing boat tied off next to the one that would eventually become Charlie's. Her brother couldn't be more than sixteen in the photo. His grin matched their grandfather's as they stood arm in arm, squinting in the summer sun.

"What do you think?" Dad asked, a tear sliding down his ruddy cheek.

"It's perfect," Rylee whispered. She handed him her bouquet then picked up the frame. "We miss you both."

She pressed a kiss to the glass, leaving a faint lipstick imprint near Charlie's cheek. Their family had endured heartbreaking losses. Family dinners, weddings and birthday celebrations would always have empty chairs left behind by Charlie and Grandpa's absence.

Sam and his family had added a framed black-and-white photo of Lucas and Erin to the table as well. Rylee's heart squeezed. With Lexi's help, Rylee had already planned an entire gallery wall of family pictures for the home she'd share with Silas and Sam. It wasn't possible to undo the tragedies that had taken their loved ones far too soon, but she and Sam would keep telling Silas great stories. Grief had taught her that a strong legacy of love and faith were priceless gifts.

"My dad and Charlie would be so happy for you." Dad's voice pulled her back to the present. He wiped his hand across his face and gave back her bouquet. "Let's not keep Sam waiting any longer."

She nodded and then waited while Tess adjusted the train on her dress one more time.

It had been a long journey from doubting she could ever love anyone again, to being just steps away from walking down the aisle. She'd been so afraid and so ashamed of her fear when she'd first met Sam. But God had never abandoned her. Instead, He'd covered all of her doubts and fears with His boundless grace. And reminded her that He was a God of second chances. She'd not only met the man of her dreams but she'd become a mother to Silas. Now she managed Hearts Bay's division of Frazier Aviation and Sam had relocated his foundation to Orca Island. The back doors of the church swung open and the organ began the processional. Rylee's body hummed with anticipation. She couldn't wait to become Sam's wife. They were blessed beyond measure.

* * * * *

Dear Reader,

One of the highlights of creating an entire series is seeing how the characters grow and change from book to book. I've enjoyed writing about all the Maddens and the secondary characters in Hearts Bay, but Rylee Madden is one character who challenged me on this creative journey. She's bold yet sassy. Not afraid to work for what she wants and is quick to give her opinion but doesn't want to accept her friends' or her sisters' advice. Perhaps Rylee's story was difficult to write because I had to confront some of my own issues with stubbornness and pride.

Isn't it interesting how God uses fictional stories and imaginary settings to teach us invaluable lessons? Writing Sam and Rylee's story reminded me of God's promise that we cannot live this life by our own strength alone. He is always with us, even when we're stubborn and trying to do things our way. As always, my hope is that reading *A Baby in Alaska* will inspire you to reflect on the truths found in God's word and strengthen your relationship with Him.

Thank you for supporting Christian fiction and telling your friends how much you enjoy our books. I'd love to connect with you. You can find me online: https://www.facebook.com/heidimccahan/, https://www.heidimccahan.com/ or https://www.instagram.com/heidimccahan.author/. For news about book releases and sales, sign up for my author newsletter: https://www.subscribepage.com/heidimccahan-newoptin.

Until next time,
Heidi